Morgan Dix

Harriet Starr Cannon

A memoir

Morgan Dix

Harriet Starr Cannon
A memoir

ISBN/EAN: 9783337092757

Printed in Europe, USA, Canada, Australia, Japan

Cover: Foto ©Raphael Reischuk / pixelio.de

More available books at **www.hansebooks.com**

Very Sincerely Yours.

+ Harriet.

M. Sup. Com. S. M.

Harriet Starr Cannon

FIRST MOTHER SUPERIOR

OF THE

SISTERHOOD OF ST. MARY

A BRIEF MEMOIR BY

MORGAN DIX

SOMETIME PASTOR OF THE COMMUNITY

TRINITY MISSION HOUSE

NEW YORK

LONGMANS, GREEN, AND CO.

LONDON AND BOMBAY

1896

PRELUDE.

OF all the views on the line of the Hudson River, none, perhaps, is more striking than that presented at the point where the stream, escaping from the compression of the Highlands, expands into the broad inland lake known from old time as the Tappan Sea. Through the mountain range, cloven ages ago by some vast glacial movement or convulsion of nature, the impatient waters have forced a passage, until, as if with a sensation of relief, they pour down upon the level land, catching, perhaps, the first sound of welcome from the ocean towards which they now draw rapidly and joyously forward. The scene at the point referred to arrests and charms the eye. On the right hand, like an outer bastion, stands a great round-topped mountain ; to the left, where the shore is indented by a deeply recessed bay, appears the village of Peekskill shut in by defending hills. The ridge to the north of that village lifts a dense foliage into the air ; and above the masses of maples, cedars, and chestnuts, may be descried what seems to be the bell tower of some church or chapel hidden from sight and crowning the plateau. The structure to which the tower belongs, and whatever other buildings may be there, remain invisible until the traveller has climbed the heights on which they stand, and passed through a wide gateway into an enclosure of some fifty or sixty acres presenting as he advances one object after another apt to fix the attention. A broad avenue commands the prospect over the low country, the valley in which the village stands, and the inland lake ; one building after another is reached and passed, until the chapel is disclosed to which the tower belongs. Built on the rock of the plateau, itself as it were a part of the ledge, it reminds one of the church at Assisi, having, like that, an upper and a lower church, the former spacious and of noble proportions, the latter a mortuary chapel, where the Offices of the Dead are statedly sung, and to which the bodies of the faithful departed are taken to await the time of burial. Beyond, as he advances, the traveller sees to the right buildings of large size, half hidden by the trees;

and, first, the school known as St. Gabriel's, from whose door it is probable that a troop of merry girls may come fluttering forth, taking their way to favourite woodland paths for recreation; still further appears the outline of the great Mother House of the Community of St. Mary, where dwell the head of the Order, some twenty Professed Sisters and Minors, and a score at least of Novices. If now the pilgrim to this home of religion, art, and letters, leaving the Chapel on his right hand, should walk some distance northward, he will come to a level field, or dell, surrounded by rocky heights, the resting-place of some who have passed beyond these earthly lights and shadows. The grass-grown mounds which break the surface of the ground are without headstone, name, or inscription ; on each is a simple cross ; nothing indicates what traveller may here have reached the end of the journey, what weary frame is sleeping here in the peace of God; nor need this be known, save to the Community, as one by one their dead are brought here to burial.*   But

---

* Since writing this paragraph, I am informed that Mr. Le Grand Cannon of New York has made arrangements to erect a cross in the cemetery at St. Gabriel's, as a memorial to his kinswoman, to bear her name and an appropriate inscription.

it may be questioned whether anywhere else on earth a deeper impression of the restfulness of holy death is made upon the thoughtful observer. All is still; no sound of the outer world disturbs this repose; the trees wave in the wind; the cliffs look down upon the place; lights and shadows fall, in course, across it as days and nights come and go; a woodpath leading from the side of the convent passes on to a point whence may be seen the great river flowing steadily towards the sea; not far away is a grove of pines, where, of a summer evening, the wanderer may rest, and see beyond him the military camp-ground of the State, and hear at sunset the call of the bugle and the evening gun. The sleeping place, to which we now return, seems fitted above all others for the rest of those daughters of our Lord, who having finished their course in faith, and having left there what of them could die, now expect the resurrection of the dead and the life of the world to come. It is not to be wondered at that, now and then, one trained at St. Gabriel's for her life work, and finding the end at hand in some far-off region, has longed for her own place among those sleepers, and asked, earnestly, that her body might be taken home and laid beside her sisters in the much-loved spot.

In that cemetery at St. Gabriel's, on the 9th
day of April, 1896, it being the Thursday in
Easter week, there was committed to the ground
the mortal body of one of the noblest and most
remarkable women of our day; a body once the
earthly tabernacle of a vigorous mind, a clear
intellect, a resolute will, and a great heart full
of love to God and man. The world knows little of her and cares less; her life work was not
that which this generation applauds; the object
for which she lived makes no appeal to the rest-
less spirits of our day; but if ever God's work has
been done well and faithfully it was so done by
that active brain, that devoted heart, those hands
that never tired, those feet which trod for forty
years the path of close and closer walk with the
Lord. As if by His special and most gracious
mandate, she was called out of this world on
Easter Day; at half-past three in the afternoon the
exodus was made; four days later the precious
body was committed to the ground, in the midst
of those nearest and dearest to her on the earth,
a great number of sisters, associates, priests, and
devoted friends assisting at the solemn action.
After the due performance of the Rites of the
Church, in long procession, carried on the shoul-
ders of four priests, followed by her spiritual

children, and by many clergy from our own and
distant dioceses, she was borne to the grave.   It
was remarked, and none could fail to notice, that
the season, which had been backward, seemed to
have changed suddenly; the voice of the spring-
tide and the first prophecy of summer were in the
air ; the sun shone brilliantly on the little procession; light breezes stirred the trees; and, for the
first time that year, the birds began to sing, as if
joyfully praising the Lord.   Unseen forms must
have been also in attendance; visitants from another realm, to whose presence may have been
due some of that impression of awe and wonder
with which we withdrew from the scene.

And now that all is over on this side, and now
that she has been received out of our sight, it
has been felt that some memorial, some written
record, should be prepared of greater length
than those which have already appeared in the
journals of the day, commemorative of that life.
This seems desirable for many reasons; as a trib-
ute to the woman who was with us once as a
burning and a shining light; as a statement of the
motives of her action during a long and memorable life; as a record of the results of the indomitable energy with which she wrought, and the
reward of patience and faith conceded to her lov-

lng service; as a history of the varied experience, through which, in evil report and good report, in reproaches, misunderstandings, and opposition, she steadily pursued her way; as a gift to those of the Community founded by her, which may serve for reminder, encouragement, and warning, as they carry on the work which throve so wonderfully under wise and strong leadership, and now devolves on them the weight of an unspeakably grave responsibility. Such purposes might a memoir serve which was all that it should be; therefore the writer could wish that the task of preparing it had been laid on some one more worthy than he. There are men and women in the Church far better fitted for this undertaking, though in one point he yields to none of them; in his devotion to that blessed memory, his appreciation of that mission of which she was the apostle, his profound reverence for the manner in which her work was accomplished, his earnest desire that every thought of hers respecting it may be fulfilled. It is nearly a quarter of a century since, as Pastor of the Sisterhood of St. Mary, he knew, in the sacred intimacy of the priestly office, all that its Superior was planning, desiring, suffering. Others, since that distant day, have done the work which he was compelled to lay down, but the afterglow is bright on the skies behind us, and through that light it may be given him to write down something apt to help and teach, to remind those who were then her companions, to help those who shall come after.

> " So be it: there no shade can last
>   In that deep dawn beyond the tomb:
>   And bright from marge to marge shall bloom
>   The eternal landscape of the past."

We move, like shadows, between a past full of visions and dreams of good, and a future where in substance these visions and dreams are to turn to unchanging realities in the heavenly city.

BIRTH AND EARLY YEARS.

SO now let us take our work in hand, and show what God wrought, in one conse-crated life, in those seventy-four years, between 1822 and 1896. What years they have been, whether we look upon them from the secular side or from the precincts of the Kingdom of Heaven! How strong the contrast between the action of the Spirit of God in souls and hearts reverent of the truth, and aiming at union with Him and fulfilment of His will, and the working of the Spirit of the Age, in souls equally in earnest but misled by the chimeras of the day and dreaming of progress apart from religion! We have seen, and are now seeing, strange sights; revolts and revolutions, the phantasmagoria of experiment, the agitation caused by morbidly sensitive and nervous men and women, crazed by excitement, and stimulated by the wish for the

impossible: and this we recognize as the work of
the Zeit Geist.   On the other hand we see a revival of the life hidden with Christ in God: fruits
of divine charity; building on a sure foundation;
help meet for a world which lives in God and cannot get away from God: plainly the work of that
Lord whom it is light and joy to follow and sin
unpardonable to reject and deny.   My story is
that of a woman's life, led in the grace of the
Gospel, and growing from more to more; a woman
who turned her talents to account for the Master
of the house; who exalted the ideal of true womanhood; who saw, first and always, the overruling
Providence which guides the course of time, who
was reverent of the Supernatural, and strong in
that faith which is the substance of things hoped
for, the evidence of things not seen.   Had it been
possible for such a thought to pass through her
humble mind, she might have appropriated to
herself the saying of the Ever Blessed, '' For He
that is mighty hath magnified me : and holy is
His Name.''

My story begins with that of the Cannon family,
of which the progenitor emigrated from France
early in the 17th century.   The Cannons were a
family of rank and wealth, Huguenots by religion,
and, for that reason, refugees; passing first into

Holland, thence to England, and thence to the
Colony of New Netherland, into which they came
about the year 1632. We have few details of their
history for the first fifty years; no record can be
traced of births and deaths, but if tradition may
be trusted they held a high social position in the
town and province. The first authentic record
brings before us John Cannon, then known as
"Jean Canon," a merchant in the city of New
York in 1693. In 1697 he married Marie Le
Grand, daughter of Pierre Le Grand; he resided
in Pearl St. between State and Whitehall Sts.,
and carried on a large and prosperous business
until 1720, when he was succeeded by his son John.
Le Grand Cannon, son of John, and grandson of
the first John Cannon, a distinguished man of his
day, resided for many years in Stratford, Conn.,
and died there in 1789. Further information on
the subject of this family may be found in the
New York Biographical and Genealogical Regis-
ter, in Orcutt's work on Stratford, and in Valen-
tine's Manual of the Common Council of New
York for 1864, in which latter work, in a list of
baptisms in the Dutch Church, 1697 to 1720, appear the names of several children of John (or
Jan) Cannon. The names of Pintard and Scher-
merhorn also occur in this large connection. I

have before me a drawing of the family coat-of-arms; the field has a figure of an artilleryman, in the costume of 150 years ago, applying a lighted fuse to an equally old-fashioned gun; for a motto, the words, *Firmior quo Paratior*. An old family Bible containing records of the Cannon family was long in the possession of the late Reverend Mother Superior; she sent it, in 1892, to her kinsman Le Grand B. Cannon, Esq., of 311 Fifth Avenue, New York. From a letter of his, acknowledging the gift, I am permitted to make the following extract:

" I duly received this morning (Dec. 15, 1892) your kind note announcing your Xmas present, and by special messenger your gift of the Old Family Bible, and also your photograph and Dr. Dix's letter.

" I greatly prize the gift, as quite independent of its antiquity and family associations, the impulse which governed you in making me its inheritor and possessor enhances the value of the gift ; and for all this you have my earnest thanks.

" The condition that your own mortuary shall be the last record in the Bible will be observed if I survive, or the obligation transmitted to my son."

In the early part of this century in the city of Charleston, South Carolina, lived William Can-

FIRMIOR QUO PARATIOR

non and Sally his wife. Mr. Cannon was the son
of Lewis Le Grand Cannon; his wife, Sally Hinman, was the youngest daughter of Isaac Hinman.
Two daughters were born to them, Catharine
Ann, Sept. 23, 1821, and Harriet Starr, May 7,
1823. On or about the 24th day of November,
1824, both parents died at Charleston, of yellow
fever, leaving the little girls helpless and all but
alone among strangers. Fortunately, Capt. James
Allen, brother-in-law of Mrs. Cannon, arrived in
the port of Charleston about that time, on a trad-
ing voyage in his own sailing packet; having been
advised of what had occurred, he found the children, living, but divested of everything that they
possessed, and in a position of great danger.
They were taken at once on board the vessel,
and brought to Bridgeport, Conn., where they
were gladly received by Mrs. Fowler, their aunt,
a sister of their mother's, and taken to that home
which was thenceforth theirs until they attained
to womanhood.

The children received a good education, and
were carefully brought up. Their attachment to
each other appears to have been singularly strong
and devoted. Harriet is described as a girl of
lovable disposition, and attractive and charming
manners, a general favourite, always bright and

cheerful, making every place happy in which she appeared. She was a proficient in music, and gave lessons in that art to the children of her relatives and friends.

Time passed on; and in 1851 the elder sister Catharine was married to Mr. John Ruggles, and went out to California, to make her home on the Pacific coast. Her one desire appears to have been that Harriet, her beloved sister, should be with her; arrangements to that end were made, and all was ready when, only a week before her departure for the West, the fatal tidings came that Mrs. Ruggles was dead. This was in 1855. The blow overwhelmed the survivor of that devoted pair. It formed the crisis of her life. Left, as she felt herself to be, alone, her purposes defeated, her plans broken off, and herself free to take her own course in the world, she little knew that God, in the mysterious order of His Providence, was drawing her away from earthly ties, and nearer to Himself. Vocations are determined in many and diverse ways. Some go to God, from the unclouded brightness of happy morning hours ; some through the heavy shadow of sorrow; some after bitter trial of the instability of temporal things, and some without one painful memory to darken the retrospect. In this case it was intense sorrow which prompted action. The penumbra of that sorrow lay, for many years, upon the chastened soul. In a letter written thirty-one years afterwards, she recurs most touchingly to her bereavement. Writing from St. Gabriel's, June 28, 1886, to one of the Community, she says :

" I have your plaintive letter; and I feel that I know it all, that I understand it all; at the same time I know that you are ready to learn the lesson God would have you to learn; that He has given the loneliness only that He may fill the void with a double portion of His Spirit. I can look back to one period of my life when I scarcely knew whether the sun rose or the sun set; when for days there seemed to be no one in the world but myself. That time was, when God took to Himself my only sister, whom I loved with a love which words can hardly express, for she was my all. Having neither father nor mother nor brother, we were almost like one person. God had a purpose for me. Had she lived, I doubt if I could have had the courage to respond to His purpose. God in His good time will show you too what He would have you to do and to be, because of this voice."

In another letter she refers to the same subject, as dwelling on a life-long and vivid memory.

" Aug. 12, 1887.

" *My dearest Sister:*

"A thousand thanks for your dear note. The day it reached me I was thinking of the events of fifty years ago, events brought to my mind by an invitation to be present at a ' Golden Wedding.' I remembered (I was just fourteen then) how I stood in a certain spot to witness the marriage ceremony. Oh how little do we know what our lives are to be! We plan for one manner of life, while God plans for us altogether another plan of life. It is a great rest to me never to have doubted His will in my regard. It cannot be long now before I shall go to Him, before ' I shall see Him as He is.'

" Ever lovingly yours,
" THE MOTHER."

It may be inferred from these letters that some thought of a dedication of her life to the immediate service of God had been in the heart of this young girl; an idea yet crude, an immature purpose. But the crushing sorrow cleared up the matter; she saw her way, she took her course; she held it thenceforth, steadfastly, step by step, as the Spirit led on, even unto the end.

Assured, now, that the Lord had called her, she began to look about and consider how and where to find the means of obeying that summons. And here, in the record of her life, we come upon the figures of a man and a woman, noted in their day, who helped her, and left the impress of their influence upon her career. Let us turn to them, and see how the strands of those three life histories were woven together, and how, later on, these faithful servants of the Master drifted apart, when the Divine purpose had been fulfilled.

2

III.

FIRST ESSAY IN A SISTER'S LIFE.

A T the time of which I write the Church of the Holy Communion, on Sixth Avenue and Twentieth St., was one of the most important centres of Church work in the City of New York. Its Pastor was William Augustus Muhlenberg, of blessed memory, one of the great powers of his day. Dr. Muhlenberg may be said to have had at heart two things above all others : the extension of charitable work among the poor, and the restoration of visible unity among the Christian bodies around us and their unification in one Catholic Church. He was the founder of St. Luke's Hospital, a magnificent monument to his memory, an institution which will be, to the end of time, associated with his name. The Church of which he was the Pastor, and which was built for him, was regarded, at that time, or rather somewhat before that time, with the same apprehension with which people now look upon the ritualistic churches of our day ; it was the " advanced " parish of the moment. Dr. Muhlenberg loved the beautiful in the externals of religion ; music, architecture, ceremonial, and all that makes divine worship impressive. I have heard old men who were scholars of his at College Point long before he came to New York, describe the services in the chapel at that place, and tell how they used to hold their Christmas Matins at early dawn, the place fragrant with incense, the picture of the Madonna and Child above the altar decorated with flowers, and the service sung, with carol and chant, in Latin.* There was much in all this to attract, delight, fascinate the ardent souls of the young, who no doubt imagined beneath this exterior some things which did not exist. For to say that Dr. Muhlenberg had his limitations is to say what might be said of most great and holy men. His theology was rather of the Lutheran than the Anglican type. In his devotion to the cause of Christian unity he might perhaps have taken down some defences which to others appear necessary to the safety of

* On the ritualism and services in the school, see "The Life of Dr. Muhlenberg," by Miss Anne Ayres, pages 18, 148.

our own Church. Beautiful as was the order of
the services, he stopped short of the sacramental
system as taught by the Oxford school; and he
had no sympathy with views in advance of the
point which he had reached in working out his
own parochial, liturgical, and charitable ideal.
I do not write this in disparagement of that noble
soul, that great heart, but because the fact has a
bearing on the story which I am telling, which
will presently appear.

It was fitting and right for an ardent nature,
filled with love for God and man, and seeking the
way of complete dedication to our Lord, to turn
to William Augustus Muhlenberg as the one who
might be supposed to know more about the ways
and means thereto than any other man. It was,
above all, natural for a woman like Harriet Starr
Cannon to look to him, because he had already
taken a new departure in the line of woman's
work in the Church. It was a part of the original
scheme of St. Luke's Hospital, that the sick in its
wards should be nursed by women consecrated by
a religious motive and special obligations to the
performance of that duty. Another jewel in the
crown of that good man was that he gave the first
impetus to the cause of Sisterhoods in our Church.
He had already organized a little band of women

for that purpose : regardless of the fears and prejudices of the time, he had boldly called them by the title of Sisters : the " Sisterhood of the Holy Communion." As the work of the Hospital grew, recruits for these nursing sisters, or as we should now style them, Hospital Nurses, were in demand ; and devout women were readily and gladly admitted to the number. The principal spirit in this little band was Anne Ayres, " Sister Anne," as she was called, a woman as remarkable in her way as the Pastor of the Holy Communion in his. Here then were all that Harriet Cannon needed : a place in the Church, a work to do among the poor and needy; the supervision of a spiritual father ; the help and animating influence of a woman of undoubted sanctity and larger experience, as guide to the higher life. She made application and was kindly received. After some test she was enrolled in the Sisterhood : she writes (**Feby. 7,** 1888):

" Yesterday was the 6th of February; the 6th of February, 1856, was also Ash Wednesday. On that day I was received as a candidate for the Sisterhood of the Holy Communion, in the Oratory of the Sisters' House and by Dr. Muhlenberg; just 32 years ago, and I was then thirty-two years old."

On the Feast of the Purification, Feby. 2, 1857, she was admitted into full membership, in the new Sisterhood, and there, in the parish and in St. Luke's Hospital, she worked assiduously and lovingly for nearly seven years.*

The years thus spent brought practice and experience ; they brought something else, the impression, dawning dimly, growing slowly, but attaining finally to full conviction, that what Sister Harriet wanted she had not found, and was not in the way to find. She had, no doubt, from the first her own ideal of life work; it could not be realized in the position in which she now found

* The following incident is related by Anne Ayres in the Life of Dr. Muhlenberg : it occurred in the Infirmary connected with the Church of the Holy Communion, when a malignant contagious disease had gained a foothold there : referring to Dr. Muhlenberg's frequent visits to the ward, she goes on to say :

"On one of these occasions he found a young probationary Sister, rocking, as he lay wrapped in a blanket within her arms, a little boy very ill with the loathsome disease. She was singing a hymn for him, and the poor child smiled as he looked up to her face, and forgot his pain and restlessness. Dr. Muhlenberg came down from the ward enamoured of the picture—'The very ideal of a Sister of Charity.' It was Sister Harriet." (See p. 276 of the "Life.")

herself. The works of Christian charity do not lie on the same level, there are grades in that department of human activity as in all others; ruder forms, and complete organisms towards which the lower naturally lead the way. From the woman of the world, who gives what of time she can spare from its pressing demands to some benevolent institution or charitable society; thence to the Bible reader or parish visitor, who, living on her modest little salary, devotes so many hours *per diem* to looking up and ministering to the poor of her district ; and on to the Deaconess, or member of the parochial Sisterhood who serves with a fuller consecration and yet with reservations ; step by step may women pass till they reach a point of unreserved surrender when the world and its concerns are left behind as completely as though they were dead to it and it was dead to them. Such progress will be accounted legitimate by the wise ; each grade has its own grace and merit ; yet some are lower and some higher ; there are here, as elsewhere, a first and a last. The highest point of all was that at which Sister Harriet was aiming ; like a dream of good it possessed her mind and soul. The idea of a life of complete and unconditional surrender to our Lord, led by a number of women in community,

bound to God by vow, and to each other by a Rule,
forming a family and a household, governing
themselves, under the sanction of Church author-
ity but holding no allegiance to earthly master,
board, or trustee, or to any other but the Sov-
ereign Himself ; realised in institutions for carrying on all works of mercy that woman can do, and
living a retired, sacramental life, in abstinence,
discipline, prayer, and constant worship : this was
the end of aspirations and desires which nothing-
ing less could satisfy and fill. Already such
organizations could be seen, in England ; the
great and growing communities at Clewer, East
Grinstead, and elsewhere ; the thing was no
dream but an accomplished fact ; why should not
fruits of faith like these grow on our American
vine ? That this ideal was not to be realized
where she was, became year after year distinctly
evident. Not that a person was wanting to lead
such a movement. The remarkable woman who
was known as " First Sister " in the Sisterhood
of the Holy Communion had the qualities which
fit for headship ; she might have made an Abbess,
with iron will and hand. But Sister Anne Ayres
had also her limitations ; her sympathies were not
with those who desired to reproduce the Anglican, or, let us say, the Catholic, type of the Re-

ligious Community in this country and in our Church : her ideal of woman's work was of a less pronounced and more free type. In this respect also she was in accord with the man whom she venerated above all others in this world. Reading what she has written, we see the perfect harmony, the singular unity in view, opinion, and mode of action, between the head of the Sisterhood and the venerable priest who had founded it.* The Sisterhood of the Holy Communion, if it was to continue and grow, must grow on lines which they approved ; no one could serve there unless in accord with the two who had begun and would direct the movement. This was the position in which certain ladies found themselves who had joined it with different aspirations : they saw themselves barred out from the hope of realizing

* The views of Dr. Muhlenberg on the subject of Sisterhoods are given fully, and, I doubt not, with perfect correctness, in the very interesting volume entitled " The Life and Works of William Augustus Muhlenberg," by Anne Ayres. (New York, Harper & Brothers, 1880.) It seems that he approved of them, " not as ecclesiastical organizations but as simple evangelical associations " ; he thought that they ought not to exist as corporations in the legal sense of the term, nor to have a central government, nor to be bound by any vow or rule, nor ever to hold property in their own right. (See page 251 *et seq.*)

what was to them the complete ideal of the Religious Life. They came to that conclusion in great
sorrow and distress; but they came to it as one
which was inevitable. Watching them, at that
moment, we sympathize with their discomfiture:
we do more ; we feel, that as there are many
operations of the same Spirit, so it must be, in this
world, that some are called to work on one line
and some another. I will venture another suggestion. No society is patient of two very strong
and very positive heads. It is impossible to imagine the woman whose career we are considering as passing her life as a hospital nurse, or
a semi-detached deaconess ; she had abilities,
powers, a mind, a will, marking her out for
larger things : she was called of God to greater
work. One cannot imagine two such strong char-
acters as Sister Anne Ayres and Sister Harriet
Cannon dwelling together harmoniously in the
somewhat indefinite relation of a parochial society. It was inevitable, it was for the best, that
they should part, each taking her own way according to her conscience and her light.

There were other women in the same position
as Sister Harriet; women moved by the same desire of consecrating themselves in the true Religious Life; women who had been attracted to the

work of St. Luke's Hospital and had come to join the labourers there. Such as these had every facility for working among God's poor, where they were; but beyond lay something which they perceived that they could not attain. They had been drawn into a position from which they must retire; the alternative being to remain at the sacrifice of the promptings of conscience, the strong desire for an advance, and the mature conviction of their enlightened understanding.

The end came in the year 1863. Some troubles which had existed for a considerable time then came to an issue, and the First Sister resigned. She appears to have done so because she thought that her ideas in regard to governing the other Sisters were not approved by most of them. She said to one of them, who recorded her words at the time: " There were only two things for me to do—either to rule with greater strictness than before, or to withdraw. I chose the latter course." Her companions, distressed at her action, refused to accept her resignation ; but Dr. Muhlenberg, to whom the matter had been referred, gave sentence that the Sisterhood had been dissolved by the withdrawal of its head, and proposed that its members should now form themselves into " a Company of Christian Ladies, and work under

1435

Miss Ayres as Matron of the Hospital." Four
of the little band found themselves more closely
united than ever by this action, and more earnestly resolved to find the way to the goal which
they were seeking. In sorrow they relinquished
the work in which they had been happy and hopeful, and went back to their own homes; not aban-
doning their faith in the Religious Life and their
longing for it, but not knowing how, or when, or
where they were to attain the desire of their soul.
They went out not knowing whither they went,
but strong in faith in Him who is invisible.

The sorrows and disappointments of that day
belong to a distant era, and the grave has closed
over nearly all the actors in that little drama.
But Christian charity soon healed the wounds, of
which not even scars remain. All was of God.
Sister Harriet spoke often and with interest of
her apprenticeship served in the Sisterhood of the
Holy Communion ; reverently and affectionately
of its saintly founder and its first head. She was
one of those who cling to early friends; never
have I heard from her one word of criticism or
unkindly comment on those with whom she first
trod the way of the Cross. When Sister Anne,
after many years spent in seclusion, was called to
her rest, the Superior of the Sisterhood of St.

Mary was among those who stood nearest to her bier, and watched with full and tender hearts the committal of dust to dust. " Blessed are the dead who die in the Lord: Even so, saith the Spirit."

IV.

THE HOUSE OF MERCY.

THERE are men who are helps, and men who are hindrances, at the turning points of life. It was fortunate for those three or four women, anxious, depressed, uncertain what to do, that they had a friend in the great bishop, Horatio Potter, who at that time was over us in the Diocese of New York. He heard of what had taken place, and came to the aid of the refugees, with the offer of a work in which they might at once engage. The House of Mercy had been founded by Mrs. William Richmond, as a reformatory for fallen women. She was a woman of indomitable energy, with an enviable faculty for obtaining money for carrying such projects into effect; and she had acquired, for the purposes of her work, the fine old Howland mansion, which stood at the foot of 86th Street on what is now the Riverside Drive. This property, including the

large house and some twelve city lots, was held
for her by trustees ; a very valuable purchase ;
and there some forty or fifty unfortunates, for
the most part young, were housed and cared for,
in the hope of converting them from the path of
sin and bringing them home by the way of peni-
tence, to the great Shepherd of souls. But Mrs.
Richmond, incessantly engaged in raising the
means to carry on the institution, and most of the
time absent, could give no attention to the task
of ruling and directing a class so turbulent and
desperate as that within the high enclosures of
the House of Mercy, where, indeed, things were
in a state of confusion. The Bishop of New
York, deeply interested in the work, and perceiv-
ing the need of able and competent governors of
those wild waifs of civilization, bethought him of
the three or four women who, having been trained
in St. Luke's Hospital, and being then desirous
of an opportunity to resume their labours in some
mission field, might be open to a call to that hard
and delicate service. The result was an invitation to take charge of the House of Mercy ; its
glad acceptance; and the prompt appearance of
Sister Harriet and her companions at the institution. In all this they were cordially welcomed
and aided by the noble-minded foundress of the
House. This was in September, 1863.

When the Sisters took charge of the House of Mercy, they were desperately poor : the sum allowed to each of them for their support, from the common fund, was only eight cents per diem. The work was difficult and trying; it had, however, a comical as well as a serious side. The Howland mansion, like old-fashioned dwellings of an earlier age, was one of those which ghosts might haunt and in which strange sights might appear. From the entrance, flanked with lofty columns, one entered a very large hall, surrounded by rooms of proportionate size, used as parlors, reception-rooms, dining-room, etc. Out of the hall a broad staircase led to the stories above. One of the rooms on the hall floor was turned into a chapel. As the day went away, the old place took on a shadowy and weird look. Among the rooms were some which could be lit up only by the help of candles; dark shadows hid much from view ; children could have found no better place for hide-and-go-seek; uncomfortable sensations were not wanting ; the occasional rat might go scooting boldly from one dark corner to another. In this old-fashioned place Mrs. Richmond had collected a considerable number of girls from the streets of New York. They were wild as hawks, impatient of constraint, often dangerous, and always planning the means of escape. Such was the place, and such the charge of which these women had undertaken the interior government. In a very short time results began to appear. Strong hands, loving hearts, compassionate souls took up the case of these unfortunates, in the Name of Christ ; under the influence of the new, and to them strange, power, the more violent spirits were curbed and refrained ; order began to take the place of disorder ; the acts of religion, if they did not yet avail to change the hearts, at least compelled a reverence for holy things to which these unhappy creatures had been strangers. Nothing is so discouraging as the work of reformation of fallen women ; evil passion were enough of itself to wreck the moral nature, but to this must be added the craving for strong drink which always accompanies lust ; until the physical system becomes impregnated with vile potations to such a degree that it seems next to impossible to revive the moribund powers of conscience and the wish for reform. In the noble army of Christian workers, the honourable position of forlorn hope is held by those who labour for the reclamation of the fallen and lost.

From one of those who went at that time to the

3

House of Mercy, and worked there till transferred
to another field, I recently received a pleasant account of the life of the Sisters at that place, and
their varied difficulties in carrying out their trust.
This I shall transcribe, as an original contribu-
tion to this history. It will be observed that she
speaks of Sister Harriet as "the Mother," though
she had not then the title or the office. It will
also be observed by what steps and by what judi-
cious measures the work was brought into shape.
Some of these reminiscences relate to days much
later than those of which I am writing; but they
help to fill out the picture and inform the reader
of the mode in which the reform proceeded.

"The life of Mother Harriet at the House of
Mercy was, from the beginning, marked by a
strict devotion to duty. Her great kindness of
heart, courtesy of manner, and good judgment
led the rest of us to look to her for guidance in all
matters of difficulty. Unfailing patience with the
infirmities of others, and even with their serious
faults, was one of her marked characteristics;
things should be set right rather than punished.
She had that flexibility of character which
smooths difficulties. The lovely traits of Mother
Harriet's character were, perhaps, nowhere more
apparent than at the House of Mercy. She possessed, as few do, the faculty of discovering what
is best in every one and bringing out the bright

side of every person with whom she came in contact. She seldom found fault in words ; a dis-
pleased look and silence had oftentimes more
effect than anything she could have said; and the
impression given was, ' I leave all entirely in
God's hands.' She was ready to measure the
capabilities of those who with her were devoting
their energies to the good of the unfortunate inmates in the House. What could each do to secure the best results in the work ? This was to
be tested. The Mother shrank from no work
however menial that work might be. She showed
that rare quality which was so evident in all her
after life,—of assigning to each one the work best
fitted for her. Those who were with her well
remember her industry. Great and absorbing as
the mental work was, her hands were never idle.
Her self-denying acceptance of the actual poverty, which at first existed at the House of Mercy,
when the Sisters were deprived of what are usu-
ally called the necessaries of life, and the unfailing humor that enlivened those days of straitness
and want, has formed the stock of many amusing
stories related by the Sisters to those of subsequent times. A merry heart makes a continual
feast; it was indeed true of her. Her influence
over the unfortunate inmates was very soon felt.
Her unfailing amiability, her strong faith in the
good in another's heart, in spite of the sin of
which that heart may be guilty; her winning sympathy, her beautiful example of true devotion to
her ever-present Lord, could not fail to attract.
Many of those whom she influenced in those early
days, thirty years ago, have stood loyal to her
through all the changes of their subsequent lives;

and among the great number of persons who gathered at her grave, it is joyous to think were some of those penitents, whom she had won for the Master's glory.

" Mother Harriet's poverty of spirit was always marked by her acceptance of what was inferior whenever a choice was given to her. It was touching to find after her death, that of the garments which came to hand to clothe her many were those of departed Sisters, which she had preferred to use instead of new ones.

" It was our custom to hold three services, morning, noon, and evening; the last just before retiring. Mother Harriet, being passionately fond of music and possessing a beautiful voice, led the singing at these services, in which the girls heartily joined.

" The ringing of the chapel bell was the signal for the girls to run away; among their various hiding-places, the cow-house (for in those days we kept a cow) was the place best adapted for that purpose. The Sisters would therefore be compelled to start out in search of them and gather them into the chapel; not succeeding in getting them altogether, they were brought in late one by one. The absence of a Sister from the chapel was the inevitable sign that she was looking up some runaway girl. When the girls were left alone they would delight in getting up the greatest possible excitement to see what effect it would have upon the Sisters.

" Having no chaplain at the House at first, we were dependent upon those who would come occasionally, or else were obliged to take the girls out to service. On one of these occasions Bishop

Coxe came, and, at his request, the household was gathered together and a brief service held; it was a great comfort to the Sisters and an equally great help to the girls, and left a lasting impression.

"After the house was partly in order typhoid fever set in and six of the inmates were very seriously ill. All, however, recovered. On our first Christmas (for we took charge in September) we had the blessed privilege of having an early celebration, by the Rev. Dr. Charles Adams. That was one of the marked things to be thankful for, and we were thankful, too, for the recovery of our patients.

"As the early spring and summer came we were able to give out-door pleasures to the girls, which helped them very much, for their confinement in the House during the entire winter was a little irksome to them.

"In the early days of the Institution we did not know the best way to manage them. We gave ourselves more trouble and them more care than was really necessary. For instance, if any of the girls got away we would think it our duty to spend our time in search of them: entire days were spent by the Sisters in looking up a girl. Now, of course, it is quite different. We have only to send a description of the missing one to a police station, and she is very soon returned to us.

"After a time the order of the House was changed and the girls were separated and classified. They were promoted, as in a school, from one class to another, as they merited it. After a time they became deeply interested in the teaching; they were particularly fond of one of the Sisters, now departed ; she was of great service to them and had great success in taming and calming their unruly spirits.

" After a time it was thought best to seek some of the girls at the courts before they were committed to the Island, where the tendency was to sink lower and lower. Girls of the better class were met who would gladly commit themselves to the House of Mercy for two years or longer if necessary, to fit themselves for a respectable life; and many of the most satisfactory cases brought to the House were self-committed.

" It was the aim of the Sisters to give religious instruction at night, reading and talking, so that they might go to bed with some serious impression in mind, to drive out whatever wayward thoughts they may have had during the day.

" As the work went on, improvements were made, and means were freely given to the Sisters to enable them to carry out their plans for the good of the inmates. St. Mary Magdalene Day, the 22d of July, was looked forward to with pleasant anticipations. On that day they were taken for a drive; the carriages of Central Park, which held a considerable number, were engaged for the occasion and the day was spent pleasantly and happily by all. Their dinner was enlivened by ice-cream and a liberal amount of candy, and that day there was, above all, no work. However, the girls did not dislike to work. It was always the aim of the Sisters to bring out the encouraging and loving traits of Mary Magdalene and our Lord's deep compassion for that class, which had a great effect upon them.

" Easter and Christmas were high feasts for the girls and looked forward to with joy.   Privileges were granted and feasts given.

" In the Institution there was a class called the ' Honor Class,' to which the girls were promoted . according to their standing.   The Sister having that class under her special charge did everything within her power to work a permanent reform in those under their charge.   They had a piano ; and there would be music, reading of stories, and relating pleasant incidents.   Girls would often come back to the House and ask particularly for that one Sister, that they might tell her how well they were getting along in their better life.

" It was soon found that the girls would improve more if they had some work to perform, and to this end they were assigned to housework, laundry work, garden work, and the like.   We also had, for a time, a school where they were taught to read, for some of them were unable to do so. We found, however, that it was irksome for them to keep still for any length of time ; active work was best fitted for their life, in which they were left with no time to think.

" The House of Mercy was not only a home for that unfortunate class of girls, but it has also been a refuge and reformatory for many who were addicted to drink and unmanageable."

This is the history of the House of Mercy in its beginning.   I have only to add that it was removed from its old site, several years ago, and that a new House of Mercy stands on the Bolton Road at Inwood, a conspicuous object on a wooded height overlooking the Hudson River. The work has greatly increased; new departments have been added, and nothing has been omitted to render it complete for its various purposes. It is still served, as it has been from the time of its foundation, by members of the Sisterhood of S. Mary; no words are adequate to express the value of their assistance, and no other persons could have accomplished what they have wrought. The praise and honour for the successful labours of the last thirty-three years belong to those Sisters who had the House in their care through all that length of time.

In this connexion mention may be made of the first death in the Community. Sister Jane, one of the original five, and in charge of the House of Mercy, died there, after an illness of several months, on St. James' Day, July 25, 1868. She had an exceptional power over the girls and was devotedly loved by all who knew her. She departed at 9 o'clock in the evening, the hour when Compline is said. It is the rule that, after Compline, silence shall be kept throughout the House, no word being spoken till the morning. With an exquisite fitness, so often remarked in the histories of God's people, deep stillness, even the silence of death, fell on the House and its inmates as the

soul passed. Unseen visitants would no doubt
have helped to enforce the rule, had the survivors
ventured to break it. The hush was awful: the
Lord was in that place, and all, dead and living,
kept silence before Him.

V.

PERSECUTION.

THE successful administration of this first trust soon led to another invitation to Sister Harriet and her companions. In 1864 they were asked to take charge of the Sheltering Arms. This institution, founded by the Rev. Thomas M. Peters, D.D., stood, at that time, on the old Bloomingdale Road, at 100th St., not far distant from St. Michael's Church, of which Dr. Peters was Rector. Into this house were received children for whom there was no provision in other charitable institutions; not orphans, nor half-orphans, nor crippled, nor sick, but such as were even more destitute and helpless, owing to peculiar conditions; children of vicious or brutal parents, neglected, waifs, friendless: such as these found shelter there in the arms of Christian love.

The episode of the " Sheltering Arms " was at once painful and profitable. I shall tell the story

plainly, because it shows that the development
and splendid advance of the Sisterhood, and all
that came thereafter, were the result of the discipline of a petty persecution which they then
passed through.

But first it is to be noted, that a great step was
taken, soon after that time, in the way of organization into an incorporated society. The four
who went out from St. Luke's Hospital had been
held together thus far merely by the bond of a
personal attachment and a common aim. But
Sister Harriet felt that the time had come for settlement upon a stronger basis, and for the development of what was in the hearts and minds of
all. The aid of the Bishop of New York was
sought; he was asked whether he would sanction
the formation of a Sisterhood, to be under his own
supervision, but with the power to work out,
under rule, the full ideal of Community Life. To
this request the venerable prelate gave careful attention; a scheme was drawn up and submitted
to him ; principles were settled, broad outlines
drawn; the plan, after having been submitted to
a committee of presbyters for consideration, met
his approval; and he announced his readiness to
meet the wishes of his daughters in Christ. The
Feast of the Purification, 1865, was a memorable

day in the annals of our branch of the Church. On that day the Sisterhood of St. Mary came into existence. In St. Michael's Church, in the forenoon, five devout women were formally received by Bishop Potter, as the first members of a society for the performance of all spiritual and corporal works of mercy that Christians can perform, and for the quest of a higher life in perfect consecration of body, soul, and spirit to our Lord.* It was the first instance of the profession of Sisters by a Bishop since the time of the Reformation, in our communion : it was a step beyond any that had been taken up to that time in England. There the great Sisterhoods were not under Episcopal control, nor had they the advantage of direct Episcopal sanction. Their members were admitted by priests, and the management of their affairs was entirely in their own hands. It was the wish of these faithful women to have the Bishop for their father, and be permitted to look

* A provision embodied in the original report to the Bishop states that the work of a Sister is to be held to "include all the corporal and spiritual works of mercy which a woman may perform, and that the idea as well of a contemplative life of prayer and devotion, as of an active life of labour, be included in the office. But especially that she be devoted to the care of the sick and to the work of educating the young."

to him as their spiritual head. That wish was granted, to their great joy, and all was now happily begun in conformity with the ancient Catholic rule, that nothing be done without the Bishop.

Manifestly, some great things were to come of this beginning. Let every point be reverently noted. The day, the place, the hour have been recorded. The names of the five then professed were as follows :

> Harriet Starr Cannon,
> Jane C. Haight,
> Sarah C. Bridge,
> Mary B. Heartt,
> Amelia W. Asten.

The Feast of the Purification has been kept ever since as the anniversary of the foundation of the Society.

An act of incorporation was obtained from the Legislature of the State of New York, conferring on the new Society, in addition to the usual statutory powers, others peculiar to themselves; a special charter covering everything that could be desired for growth, government, and efficiency in work. Perhaps the most important provision was that no change may be made in the fundamental

law of the Institution without the joint consent
and approval of the Bishop of New York on the
one side and the Sisters assembled in Chapter on
the other.

The act of incorporation bears date in May,
1865; it was granted soon after the founding of
the new Sisterhood. Early in the month of September in the same year, in the sacristy of St.
Luke's Church, Hudson St., an election was held,
at which Sister Harriet was chosen, by the unani-
mous vote of her companions, to be Superior; an
office to which she was repeatedly re-elected, and
which she held on the day when she entered into
rest. Henceforth the title of " Mother " shall be
applied to her as I continue this narrative.

One word more as to the event of Feby. 2d,
1865. It illustrates the humility of Sister Harriet
and her devotion to her duties. On that day she
was engaged in nursing a child ill of the small-
pox. When the time for the ceremony at the
church arrived, she with great reluctance laid
down the child, and went off to St. Michael's.
As soon as the service was over she returned with
all speed to the church, and resumed the charge
of the little patient. In one of her letters I find
her recurring with some amusement to the incident:

" I remember the day just twenty years ago, when we five stood before the altar at St. Michael's, and how I slipped away from my small-pox patient to be professed ! ! "

A Rule was subsequently drawn up, containing the provisions necessary for carrying the design of the incorporation into effect. It owes its character to the intelligence and wisdom of the founder. It deals with the work of the Community, its form of government, its officers, and members, its mode of transacting business, its property, and the general regulation of affairs. The supreme power is vested in the Chapter, composed of professed Sisters. The Superior is a constitutionally appointed officer, chosen for a fixed term, and eligible for re-election. This is the Outer Rule. There is, in addition, an Inner Rule, which relates to the religious observances of the Community, and their devotional life and spiritual discipline.

To proceed with our narrative. The Sisters took charge of the Sheltering Arms in 1864: their connexion with it was not dissolved till 1870. In the meantime further demands upon their services were made. St. Barnabas' House, in Mulberry St. near Bleecker, an institution under the charge of the New York City Mission Society, needed an efficient interior management, and in the year

1867, on the request of that Society, it was also placed under their care. Of this latter institution they had charge for nearly two years.

In the Sheltering Arms the development of that life which the Sisterhood had so long been seeking began. The day had dawned. They recited daily offices ; they observed the seven canonical hours. One writes of that time :

" In these things a lovely trait of dear Mother Harriet was plainly seen and felt. Her deep devotion of spirit, however pressing were the labours of the day, brought peace. Her voice would sound out far beyond the little oratory, and many of the children and workers would look forward with pleasure to the Vesper hour; and eagerly would the children expect the nine o'clock service, which the Mother always led, when Ps. xv. was sung responsively. Her heart was full of love and tenderness for these poor little ones. As usual she was always seeking the comfort of others, and bearing personal inconvenience with an uncomplaining spirit."

The work at St. Barnabas' House was of a different character. Mrs. William Richmond had opened a house under that name for the temporary care of infants and homeless young mothers. The Sisters managed to take care of the infants, for a short time, at the House of Mercy, and this was the beginning of what is now an Infant Asylum.

At a subsequent date the City Mission Society opened St. Barnabas' House for homeless women and children ; of this, on the invitation of the trustees and with the consent of the Bishop, the Sisters now took charge. Women seeking employment and situations were allowed to remain there one week, until they could obtain work or be transferred to other institutions. Many who had been discharged from the hospitals were received there and cared for during their convalescence. Daily morning and evening services were held in the Chapel, and it was understood that the duty of the Sister was not only to relieve bodily wants but also to give spiritual help and aid. A work for the rescue of the fallen formed a part of the general plan. A room was hired on Broadway and 11th St., in which evening service, with short addresses and singing, was held; a carriage was in readiness; and those who could be persuaded to make an effort to forsake their evil life, were at once taken to St. Barnabas' House, received by the Sisters, and, whenever it seemed desirable, transferred to the House of Mercy. The great work done then, and ever since, to this day, at St. Barnabas' is too well known to the citizens of New York to need further description here.

During the sojourn of the Sisters at the Shel-

4

tering Arms, Mother Harriet was taken ill of
typhoid fever. Her strength, and all her powers
had been overtaxed. For many weeks the result
was doubtful. A long rest was ordered, after her
recovery, until she had completely regained her
health.

With the House of Mercy, the Sheltering Arms,
and St. Barnabas' House in their charge, the Sisters had all they could desire in the way of active
employment. And yet, if things had remained
in that position, the object of their organization
could not have been fulfilled. Those institutions
were under the charges of managing Boards and
Trustees, to whom all must defer, and by whose
wishes they must be controlled; independent action would have been impossible, and the development of their plans for the restoration of the Religious Life in Community would have depended
on the assent and approval of persons perhaps
not in sympathy with their views and intentions.
To be released from a possibly unfriendly re-
straint, and to build on their own foundation, was
necessary, if the Community was to become a
power in the Church. We think that the hand
of an overruling Providence can be plainly seen
in what next occurred. To tighten the bonds by
which they were already held was the way to

bring about a removal of the obstacles in the way
of advance, and to send these toilers once more
from quiet places, poor but free.

The trouble began at St. Barnabas' House.
The reception of the five Sisters by Bishop Potter,
the impressive scene at St. Michael's Church, and
the growth of the little society—for others had
been added to their number—at length attracted
public attention. The journals of the city had
given highly coloured accounts of the new society, its objects and aims, and the Protestantism
of the day at last took the alarm. What was this
thing thus growing up amidst us? What were
these so-called Sisters, these "nuns," these
"Romanists in disguise?" What had the
Bishop done? And what more might be coming? Was it true that there were to be Habits,
and a Rule, and Vows? Little by little, curiosity led to inspection, and inspection to serious
disquietude. The trouble began at St. Barnabas'
House. Among the most active of the trustees
was the estimable pastor of a prominent city
parish, a lovable man, of warm heart and great
zeal, but nervously sensitive to censure on the
part of the "evangelical" public. In the parish
of which he was the Rector before he came to
New York, there were many Irish Orangemen:

these good people were greatly scandalized by the discovery of little crosses engraved on the chalice and paten of the Communion service: the Rector, to propitiate them, sent the vessels to a silversmith and had the objectionable symbols carefully erased. It may be imagined with what anxiety a person of this disposition would watch the proceedings of those to whom the care of St. Barnabas' House and its beneficiaries had been intrusted. In the manner in which the services were conducted there was nothing to reprehend; nor yet in the ministrations to the poor or the instruction of the ignorant. But the question was raised : what might the Sisters be doing in the privacy of their rooms ? What prayers did they say there ? What offices did they recite ? What manuals of devotion might be on their tables ? These questions led to a formal demand that the Trustees should have the access to the Sisters' private apartments, as visitors, with the right to inspect all books and manuals used by them in their prayers, and that no books should be so used except such as were approved by the Trustees. Once satisfied that the alternative lay between submitting to such inquisitorial interference, or withdrawing from the House, they promptly made their choice, and, one morning, quietly took their few and scanty belongings and went away.

So then there were left in their charge only the Sheltering Arms and the House of Mercy. The Sheltering Arms had been recently founded, and was dependent for support on the contributions and donations of its friends among the Church people of the city. It was a popular charity; but its helpers were of that class who will aid only what pleases them, and may be easily influenced to withdraw their subscriptions. The feeling against the Sisters grew, and spread more widely on the report that they had been forced (for so the adversary put it) to leave St. Barnabas' House. And now began what amounted to a persecution on a small scale illustrating the acrimony of religious prejudice and the violence of Protestant antipathy. The Sisterhood became the object of comment, criticism, and animadversion; it was discussed in the fashionable circles of New York society; an intense curiosity to see those strange and dangerous creatures led to visits of inspection to the Sheltering Arms. Ladies of high social position took up the matter; it was no uncommon thing to see them, of an afternoon, driving thither in their handsome carriages, entering the building, demanding interviews with the Sisters, examining them as if they were wild animals in a menagerie, questioning, browbeating, catechising them, and even sometimes going so far as to pluck at their garments to see of what material they were made. Thus the excitement grew and spread, until it became apparent that the presence of the Sisters was detrimental to the interests of the institution, and that many subscriptions and contributions would be withdrawn if they continued in charge. It was impossible to resist the pressure; in due time Mother Harriet and her associates found that their presence was no longer desired; and with sad hearts and a burning sense of injustice they withdrew.

This is a pitiful story; but at this distance it awakens no regret except that religious bigotry should at any time have had such sway among us. To the Community, the persecution was most helpful; it threw them on themselves; it made some warm friends for them ; it showed them that to be done efficiently their work must be done in houses of their own, subject to no nagging interference and secure from molestation ; and so it led, under the Providence of God, to all that came after, step by step, and year by year, until now we see them, increased tenfold in number, firmly planted in half a dozen dioceses of the

Church, holders of a very large amount of valuable property in houses and land east, west, and south, having their own schools, hospitals, and Mother house ; growing in the possession of all things needed to a vastly extended work, and in favour with God and man.

Nor let me omit to add that if, at that time, the " society women " of New York displayed a spirit unworthy of themselves, they have amply atoned for the errors of that past day. Those bitter prejudices are dead, and beyond the chance of revival; a generous and gracious appreciation of all good has grown up in their place. I myself have recently seen, in the reception room of one of the finest mansions in Madison Avenue, a great assemblage of ladies of high social position brought together to meet a poor lay brother of Nazareth in quest of help for his work. I saw him face to face with that fair and friendly assemblage, in his brown habit with the knotted cord about his waist ; and I saw the generous and broad-minded Rector of St. Bartholomew's standing beside his humble brother and affectionately and earnestly speaking in his behalf. Thus hath God wrought in our time ; and blessed be His holy Name.

The storm which beat upon the Sisters at that time did its best to drive them from the House of

Mercy, as it had done from the other institutions in which they had served; but here its force was stayed and broken. Some agitation occurred, but a large majority of the Trustees had the courage and independence to stand, unshaken by the clamours and criminations of the hour. They never lost their confidence in Mother Harriet, nor did they ever consider the question of withdrawing what they had committed to her and her devoted companions. Beneath the surface ripples was a great depth of appreciation, affection, and confidence. The House of Mercy is still in the charge of the Sisters of St. Mary as it has been since the year 1863.*

* See an interesting communication in the *Church Eclectic,* of April, 1896, entitled: "Mother Harriet of the Sisterhood of St. Mary. A Sketch. By the Right Rev. George F. Seymour, D.D., LL.D., Bishop of Springfield. Young Churchman Co., Milwaukee, Wis." Dr. Seymour was Chaplain of the House of Mercy for several years, including the year 1867. He states that "when the Sisters were removed under coercion from the Sheltering Arms, in obedience to a published protest against them, with an implied threat that supplies would in future be withheld from the institution if they were suffered to remain in charge, the House of Mercy opened her arms to receive the fugitives; and then the further effort was contemplated to drive us all, sisters and chaplain, from the House of Mercy and leave us without shelter." But it failed, most fortunately for the work.

VI

ADVANCE, DEVELOPMENT, GROWTH.

WE come to the beginning of a new era in this history. It is our pleasant task to trace the growth of the work done by the Sisterhood from the time when they began to build on their own foundations, to the present day. The period is one of twenty-five years; we must pass over it as rapidly as possible.

Among the objects proposed in the summary of the duties of the Community is Christian education. Mother Harriet had this much at heart; the Sisterhood should be a praying Sisterhood, a nursing Sisterhood, a missionary Sisterhood, a teaching Sisterhood: she deemed the instruction of the young one of the most necessary and valuable of the works of faith; and to this she now addressed her efforts; the first thing to be established was a Christian School. A small house was rented in 46th St. between Fifth and Sixth

Avenues ; a few children came ; and, very mod-
estly and quietly, without parade or sensation,
the work was commenced.   The little school in
time became a great school; among the Sisters
were some women who had been trained as teachers; this was the opportunity to lift their work to
a higher plane.   No long time had passed before
it was found that they needed more room.   What
should be done ?   It happened (if that word be
appropriate to anything in this record) that a very
large house had been erected by a celebrated edu-
cator of the day, who, however, through financial
embarrassment, found himself compelled to give
up his design.   The building, just as it was completed and ready for occupation as a school, was
left on his hands, embarrassed with workmen's
liens, and fit for nothing but the use for which it
had been planned.   It was at No. 8 East 46th St.,
opposite the Windsor Hotel; a large and commo-
dious structure of about 40 feet front, and containing every appointment needed for a high class
school for girls.   On this property the Reverend
Mother looked with longing eyes but little hope;
till suddenly and unexpectedly the means were offered to her for its purchase, the liens were all paid,
and she found herself in possession of the house
and lot in fee.   To remove from their smaller quar-

ters was the work of a short time, and St. Mary's School was opened. It has increased and grown till it is now one of the largest in New York. The work of education has been developed, the standard of scholarship raised; its graduates easily pass the entrance examination for Barnard College and take creditable places among the students. The memory of Sister Agnes is cherished there; she was the head of the school for many years, and to her in great part is it indebted for its high reputation.

The house in 46th St. served also for a kind of headquarters of the Community; there the Mother resided, and there the novices were lodged and trained. A room appropriately fitted up and furnished as a chapel was used for the school services, and also for the devotional offices of the little Community, who recited the Hours there. Great was their content in having at last a dwelling apt for their uses, where they were secure from molestation, in the liberty of the daughters of God. I well remember those days, and especially the chapel services and the holy religion of the place. After some time the room was rearranged and enlarged; a painting by Father Derby was placed over the altar; other large pictures, also gifts, adorned the walls. The stalls were in-

creased in number so as to make places for some
thirty persons; the Sisters used to wonder whether
there would ever be enough to fill them; three
times the number of stalls are now in the choir
of the Church at St. Gabriel's.

The next undertaking of the Community was a
Hospital for children. A very modest beginning
was made; a house 12½ feet wide was rented at
206 West 40th St., and the work was begun.
One of the Sisters who had worked at the Sheltering Arms was called in to inspect the place and
give her opinion on its fitness for the purpose.
This Sister had become noted in the Community
for a special interest in funerals; it used to be said
of her that her patron Saint was Joseph of Arima-
thea. When a child died at the Sheltering Arms,
she would set out on foot and trudge beside the
body, accompanying it to its burial at St. Michael's cemetery, at Astoria. This good Sister,
after a careful inspection of the premises, announced that there appeared to her to be only one
serious drawback, the staircase was so narrow that
she thought it would be very difficult to carry
down the body of a large child! Notwithstanding, the little house was rented and three or four
children were received. How vastly, how wonderfully, that blessed work has grown! The out-

come of that venture of faith is seen in the large buildings having a frontage of 92 feet on West 34th St. near Ninth Avenue. These have come, one by one, in time; and now St. Mary's Hospital for Children ranks next to St. Luke's in the Hospitals of our Church in New York. It provides for 125 patients; it has already 52 endowed beds; and it is always full. The Out-door Department, which was started in 1881, has steadily increased. By a gift of $41,000 from a lady in this city a Dispensary, Mortuary Chapel, and Autopsy Room were also erected in 1894. The Hospital has been for years in the charge of Sister Catharine; one who was, as might be said, an adopted child of Sister Harriet in her youth; the wise, tender, and calm administrator of a great trust.

The next acquisition of the Community was that of the property at Peekskill-on-the-Hudson, now known as St. Gabriel's. The school in 46th St. had grown rapidly; but its progress was checked by want of accommodation, as the house had to serve, not only for the school, but also as a residence for several of the Sisters, and particularly for the Novices, who were now coming in considerable numbers. Mother Harriet looked forward to an establishment of some kind in the country; in fact it had become necessary; and she

wisely considered that the establishment of a
suburban school might be an aid to that design.
Accordingly, in 1872, they purchased a piece of
ground, about 30 acres in extent, on the heights
to the north of Peekskill, and opened a school
there by the name of St. Gabriel's. When it had
become thoroughly established, those of the Sisters in 46th St. who were not engaged in St.
Mary's School, were transferred to Peekskill, together with the entire Novitiate, and thenceforth
the Mother Superior made her residence there.
St. Gabriel's has become, in time, perhaps, the
most important of their possessions ; partly by
purchase, and partly by gifts, some of great
value, it has been enlarged and enriched, till it
now contains many buildings, with about 50 acres
of land. On entering the grounds, by a gate
opening from the highway, the visitor first sees
on the left a large dwelling house, to which the
school girls have given the name of the Castle,
and in which some of the older pupils are lodged.
To the right is another large building, known as
the Noyes Memorial Home, opened in 1889 for
the reception of otherwise homeless children from
St. Mary's Hospital, suffering from chronic ailments as well as for convalescents from long illness requiring bracing air; in that Home, given

by a widow in memory of her husband, formerly a clergyman of the City of New York, some 50 children are annually cared for. Passing on, the road takes a turn and ascends, commanding a view of the lower Hudson down to the Palisades; next appears the Chapel, to the left. Still farther on, at some distance, partly concealed by trees, is the school building, with accommodation for forty boarders; and next to it is the Convent, now too small, and always inconvenient. The grounds beyond are covered with the forest growth of many years; a tarn of small dimensions meets the eye, its northern side faced by a cliff known as St. Peter's Rock. Farther on is the Cemetery, and around and beyond are woods and thickets which afford a pleasant place of exercise, recreation, and amusement, where no annoyance need be feared and no molesting foot can intrude.

All that I have described has come by degrees, within the last twenty years or more ; another conspicuous monument of the foresight, energy, prudence, and business capacity of the head of the Sisterhood. For many years St. Gabriel's has been the point from which the whole work has been directed, the Mother Superior having her residence and office there, and thence carrying on her large and varied correspondence.

The following year, 1873, marks another epoch
in the history; then was made the first advance
beyond the limits of the Diocese of New York.
The Right Rev. Dr. Quintard, Bishop of Tennessee, sent an urgent invitation to Mother Harriet
for Sisters to take charge of a school and a charitable institution at Memphis, in his diocese. The
Mother had always an enthusiastic missionary
spirit; in a letter written several years afterwards,
I find these words:

"Bishop Worthington asks us to go to Ne-
braska; and we are asked to go to Philadelphia;
and we are asked to go to China. I hope some
day we may go to China."

Bishop Quintard's invitation, after careful consideration, was accepted, and three or four Sisters
were sent to Memphis.

I have received from one of the Sisters at Memphis, a communication, giving full and very interesting details of the beginning and progress of the
work in the South.   A part of it I insert as follows:

"Sewanee, Tenn.,
"June 22d, 1890.

"*Dear Dr. Dix:*
"Our dear Mother asks me to send you some
reminiscences of our Mother Foundress, associated with our Southern work.

" Our Mother had a deep affection for her native Southern land. Her heart was always touched by the pathetic poverty and unworldliness of its simple folk, especially the ' darkey,' and full of admiration for the fine qualities of its cultured people. She used to say ' There are two kinds of Southern ladies, the languid kind that can do nothing and the accomplished kind that can do most things better than any one else.'

" In 1869 Bishop Quintard, whom Mother had known from her girlhood, begged for the establishment of a Branch of St. Mary's in Tennessee. He brought to the Community three ladies from Tennessee, aspirants to the Religious life, and in 1873 the Southern Branch of the Community was established at Memphis. The work consisted of St. Mary's School and the charge of the Church Orphans' Home. The Mother made her first visit to Tennessee in December of that year. St. Mary's School then occupied the Bishop's residence on the west side of the little Cathedral. Mother enjoyed her visit heartily, finding much of the life new to her. She had not been South (I believe) since her childhood. During this visit Mother arranged the purchase of the property adjoining the Church on the east side, for St. Mary's School, though the permanent building was not begun till the spring of 1878 and was completed in 1888.

" Mother made nine visits to the work in Tennessee. On her second visit South she went to Mobile and spent some days with the Deaconesses in charge of the Orphanage in that city. From Mobile she went by steamboat up the Mobile River to visit her relations in Alabama, among

5

whom was her cousin, John English, whom she loved as a dear brother.

" In 1878, when the Mississippi Valley was afflicted by the terrible epidemic of yellow-fever, Mother expressed an earnest desire to go South to comfort and aid the Sisters in their overwhelming suffering and work. But this was not thought expedient by the Community. Her loving heart was almost broken by the great losses sustained at that time, especially by the death of the beloved Sister Constance. She came South as soon as the epidemic was over and spent Christmas of 1878 with us. She gladly consented to the continuance of the Southern work, enfeebled though it was by the death of all the Southern Sisters but one. During her visit to Tennessee in 1887 Mother visited Nashville and Sewanee for the purpose of selecting a locality for a country home for the Southern Community. She chose Sewanee because it was the site of the University of the South and because of its fine mountain air and scenery. The place now known as ' St. Mary's on the Mountain,' or ' The House of the Transfiguration,' was then purchased and dedicated on the Feast of the Transfiguration, 1888. The suffering and ignorance of the poor mountain people appealed strongly to the Mother's tender heart and she interested many of her personal friends in that mission work at Sewanee.''

The work in the South thus described by one of the labourers there, was undertaken with a deep sense of responsibility, but without hesitation. It seemed to be on the line of their hopes, intentions, and prayers. It has been greatly blessed, every way. Many postulants and novices have been sent to the Mother House in the North, young women of enthusiasm and devotion, and thus the gift to the Bishop of Tennessee twenty-six years ago has been returned sevenfold.

Let us turn next to New York. There is at No. 50 Varick St. a large six-story house next to St. John's Chapel, which for more than half a century was the Rectory of Trinity Church. It was built for Bishop Hobart, when the Park and neighbourhood were the Faubourg St. Germain of our city: he dwelt there and so did his successor, the Rev. Dr. William Berrian, upon whose death, in 1862, it became the residence of the present incumbent. About the year 1871, the Vestry, thinking it desirable that the Rectory should be at a more central point, proposed to the Rector a removal farther up town. To this he strongly objected, but finally assented, on condition that the ancient building should neither be sold nor leased for secular purposes but converted to some charitable use. Approving the suggestion, and acting on his advice, the Vestry of Trinity Church decided to turn the Rectory into an infirmary or Parish Hospital, for the benefit of our own poor and of others where room could be had. This

having been done, it was a question how the work
should be carried on; and application was made
to Mother Harriet for a Sister to take charge of
the new foundation, and as many more as might
be needed to help her. The Reverend Mother
hesitated as to compliance with the request; parochial Sisterhoods constitute a class by themselves;
in no sense was the Community of St. Mary a
parish organization; it formed a part of no parish;
it was responsible to the Bishop only; and experience had taught the danger of entangling alli-
ances. But considering that the Rector of Trinity
was at that time also the Pastor of the Sisters,
and in deference to his wishes for which he has
ever been dutifully grateful, consent was given.
A Sister was sent, with helpers; and thus a new
branch of the work was added in the largest and
oldest of the parishes of New York.

The annual reports of Trinity Infirmary, or
Trinity Hospital as it is now called, show a vast
amount of work done there, without compensa-
tion, for people labouring under the oppression of
sickness and passing through the valley of the
shadow of death: but no one has yet written, nor
could statistics tell, the story of the spiritual force
exerted there upon the sick in heart and the distressed in soul and spirit. The ministrations of

the Sisters to the weak, the penitent, the unhappy have been quite as abundantly blessed as those of the medical staff to the bodies of their patients. It has been emphatically a mission work ; the stories of persons who, during illness, have there been reclaimed or converted to Christ, are numerous and deeply affecting; the priests of St. John's Chapel have been daily visitors to the wards ; many they have prepared for baptism, confirmation, Holy Communion, and death ; many who entered the door with scarce a hope for this world or the next have gone forth strong in faith, new creatures in body and spirit, refreshed and well. By degrees some other branches of Christian work have been added to the Hospital service: guilds have been formed, classes instructed ; by large additions to the building, room has been gained for a beautiful Chapel, where priestly ministrations are extended to people not needing medical aid, and Retreats and Quiet Days have been conducted from season to season. All this work, large in range, and most important in a religious aspect, has been under the constant and devoted observation of the Sister Eleanor, for the last twenty-two years " Superintendent " of the Hospital.

Nor are the labours of the Sisters limited to the precincts of St. John's Chapel. For sixteen years

they have had charge of the Trinity Mission
House, labouring in the vast field between the
Battery and Chambers St., as helpers to the
Clergy stationed in that part of the parish.   It
must suffice to have made mention of this great
work, in which they have been so devotedly engaged; the glimpse will be enough for the reader,
already, perhaps, becoming bewildered with the
extent and variety of their labours.

But, to anticipate somewhat, I shall postpone
the story of Memphis, and complete this survey
of the field over which the eyes of the Mother
were constantly ranging, and to every portion of
which her great heart was hourly going out, by
mentioning their entrance into two more dioceses,
Wisconsin and Chicago.

In the year 1870, when Dr. William E. Armi-
tage was Bishop of Wisconsin, he founded at
Kenosha a School for Girls, as a memorial to his
venerated predecessor, Bishop Kemper, which was
intended to become eventually " a home for a Sisterhood for Church School teaching."   This
School, established and opened in the autumn of
that year, was carried on with difficulty and in-
different success for about seven years, when it
became obvious that something must be done to
rescue it from impending failure.

At a meeting of the Trustees, held Sept. 15, 1877, the Rev. Jas. de Koven, D.D., offered a resolution setting forth the long entertained desire of the Board that the School should be in the hands of a Sisterhood, and alleging that the time had come when a change in the management must be made. Upon the adoption of this resolution, the Bishop of the Diocese, the Right Rev. Dr. E. R. Welles, wrote at once to Mother Harriet, and received her reply as follows:

"St. Gabriel's, Nov. 8th, 1877.
" To THE RIGHT REVD. E. R. WELLES.
" *Rev. and Dear Sir:*
" I write this morning to say that, God willing, we will send two Sisters to take charge of Kemper Hall the next scholastic year. We feel that this is a great venture of faith,—still, if God calls, we must have no fears, but go lovingly forth in His Name. The Sisters whom I propose to send will, I think, in every respect prove equal to the task assigned them. I will write a line to Dr. de Koven to-day. Commending our little Community to your prayers, I am,
" Rev. Father in God,
" Faithfully yours,
" ✠ HARRIET, Mr. Supr.,
" Sisters of S. Mary."

In June, 1878, the Sisters came, and the School opened under their charge in the following September.

So great was the success which followed under the new management, that in January, 1886, the Board of Trustees vacated their office, and turned the School over to the Sisters, by the following resolution:

" The Trustees of Kemper Hall, recognizing the thoroughness of the work of the Sisters of St. Mary, and desiring to secure their permanent care of this Institution, propose the following plan to the Sisters of St. Mary :

" That the Sisters of St. Mary become the Trustees of Kemper Hall in place of the present Trustees (who are willing to resign in their favour) and thereby to be vested with all the power and obligations of the present Corporation."

This arrangement was accepted, May, 1886. The Board of Trustees now consists of the Bishop of Milwaukee, ex-officio, the Mother Superior and Sisters of St. Mary, and some one man of business ability selected by the Sisters to be their adviser when his services may be needed.

When the Sisters took charge of the School in 1878, there was a large indebtedness, with an annual deficit, for which the Trustees provided by borrowing from time to time, thus increasing the debt. To this the Sisters strongly objected. Since they became the Trustees in 1886, the situation changed ; a large part of the debt has already been paid, and the financial condition is sound. The property is beautifully situated on Lake Michigan, the incursions of which are prevented by a very large breakwater which cost a great sum to build and requires a considerable annual outlay to keep in order. The grounds are attractive, and defended by magnificent pines and cedars from the prairie winds. Many new buildings have been erected, including a large refectory, chemical and physical laboratories, studio and class-rooms, and enlarged dormitories. The School opened in 1870 with 10 boarding pupils and 3 day scholars; in 1883 it had 30 boarders, and for the last two years there have been 90 boarders besides a considerable number of day scholars. It is said, in the Report of the School, that there has never been a death among pupils resident at Kemper Hall since the Sisters took charge in 1878, nor any epidemic illness there. Such is the record of a work which God has blessed.

Of the spiritual work done at Kenosha much might be said. In that connexion occur the names of Bishops Welles, Knight, and Nicholson, all devoted to the interests of Church extension and Christian education at that centre of intellec-

tual, moral, and spiritual life in their portion of
the field: and with tender recollections we muse
of James de Koven, Lucien Lance, John J. Elmen-
dorff, who all laboured in the work and were in
their times helpers of Kemper Hall.

From several other quarters invitations have
come since that day, asking their presence and
their help.   Nearly all of these have been denied
for want of numbers sufficient to meet the demand.
How vast the force required for such a range of
labours !   It will be seen, when the reader comes
to the Story of Memphis, how this almost enthusiastic appreciation of the work of women in Community and devoted to our Blessed Lord grew so
fast and became so strong.   With heartfelt pain,
the Mother found herself at last unable to answer
Yes to the requests which poured into her office
at St. Gabriel's.   One, however, she forced herself to comply with ; it was that of the Bishop of
Chicago, the Right Rev. Dr. McLaren, who, in
1891, asked her aid in connexion with the mission
work at his Cathedral, in that enormous and most
perplexing, if not unintelligible, metropolis of the
West.   The Sisters were already established
firmly in that city.

Mother Harriet seems to have set her heart on
the settlement in Chicago, fully realizing the im-

portance of the field. A letter of hers bears on this point.

"St. Gabriel's, Peekskill, Jany. 17th.

" *My very dear Sister :*

" Shall we have a little chat over Chicago this morning ? . . . I think I appreciate fully all the points in regard to our taking up work in Chicago; and whenever it seems to be the will of God that we should make a foundation there, I shall be not only ready but *more* than ready to begin it. One might make two points:

" 1st. If through any action, or want of action, on the part of the Trustees, we should be obliged to leave Kemper Hall, that moment we would be ready for Chicago.

" The other point: Whenever the Province of Illinois is ready to send for training two or three candidates, we promise a foundation for Chicago. I say, the Province of Illinois, but, of course, I intend by that, any Western Diocese. I think when we have eight Sisters for our work at the West, we may safely assume *two* works. I consider now that we have five, as Sister F—— really came to us from the West, and it is my intention, as soon as it can possibly be done, either to return her, or a Sister in her place, for the work at the West. Now where are those candidates ? Can you not produce one or two of them ? Has Bishop —— no recruit forces ? Perhaps I ought to add a word in regard to his having other Sisters, as you mentioned the matter in your letter. Of course, if there should be other Sisters ready to go to the Bishop, and we not ready, it would be an indication that God did not intend St. Mary's for that field. The natural man has a longing for Chicago ; but the natural man must *not govern* but *be governed* by the *spiritual* man ; and so let us wait quietly for the clear light."

In the autumn of 1887 a small house was opened on the south side of Chicago in connexion with St. Clement's Church, Canon Knowles being then the priest in charge. The modest beginning grew in time to more. The Mother wrote after the settlement had been made in that city:

" I suppose Chicago is full of people of every sort and kind ; and that, even in the mission work, there comes some phase of this pressure of people. One feels like saying, Oh ! their souls ! their souls! Pray for the multitude."

The Sisters had been in that position three years and a half, when they removed to the Cathedral, and took up mission work on the west side. In 1894 they purchased the property next door to their Mission House, for $16,000, and opened a " Temporary Home for Children"; this also belongs to the Community.

With these establishments, at Kenosha and Chicago, there was now what might be considered a Western branch of the Community, as there was a Southern branch at Memphis and Sewanee. That these might become, at some future time, in part autonomous, holding a place in the Community something like that of Provinces in the Church at large, was the Reverend Mother's idea and earnest desire to the day of her departure.

Later, in the year 1886, the Laura Franklin Hospital in this city was placed in charge of the Sisters. This, I think, completes the list of the institutions, educational, eleemosynary, etc., now in their care, a wonderful list to have been written since the year 1867.

VII.

MEMPHIS.

THE story of Memphis has been told in full already ; * it must be too well known to need repetition. And yet some mention of it must be made, so great is its importance in this history. Before the memorable year 1878, many spoke against these faithful and devoted women : after that year, the tongue of calumny was silent, while men looked on with beating hearts, and eyes dim with tears. For God then gave to His faithful the crown of martyrdom; their names be-

* See a pamphlet entitled *The Sisters of St. Mary at Memphis. With the Acts and Sufferings of the Priests and others who were there with them during the Yellow Fever Season of 1878. By the Rev. Morgan Dix, D.D.* This pamphlet, privately printed, was, by permission of the Mother Superior, reprinted in *Church Work*, a monthly magazine for Church work, edited by Mrs. A. T. Twing, vol. ii., No. 12, October, 1887. New York, M. H. Mallory & Co., 47 Lafayette Place.

came sacred thenceforth, ennobled by the love
which shrinks not from death, in appalling form.
The light is still shining on the graves in Memphis, where they rest who laid down their lives
readily, joyfully, eagerly, for God, for the brethren, and for those who had no strength nor courage left; who thus filled up the measure of their
calling, and were nailed to the Cross with Him
who, for our sakes, became obedient unto death.
The sacrifice was at once accepted by all beholders
as the vindication of the immolated, the test of
their motives, and the proof of the power of their
faith.   It could not have come more opportunely.
A voice seemed to say, of them: "Thou shalt
hide them privily by Thine own Presence from
the provoking of all men: Thou shalt keep them
secretly in Thy tabernacle from the strife of
tongues."

It will be remembered that in the year 1873, on
the request of Bishop Quintard, and with the consent of Bishop Potter, some of the Sisters were
sent to Memphis, to found a school for girls, and
to take charge of an institution already existing,
known as the Church Home.   In August of that
year, a little band arrived, consisting of Sister
Constance, who was to be the Sister Superior and
to take the headship of the school; Sister Amelia,

one of the original five, Sister Thecla, who had just made her profession, and a novice known as Sister Hughetta, a young lady of a distinguished Southern family. Sister Amelia was set to work to organize the Church Home, then in deplorable disorder; a task for which she had a natural aptitude, with the advantage of her experience in the Sheltering Arms and House of Mercy; the other three were to be specially engaged in the educational work. Sister Constance * was a young woman of culture, intelligence, and ability, of great personal attractions, of exquisite grace, refinement, and loveliness of character—in short, qualified in every particular to train the daughters of the South, of whom a considerable number were at once readily confided to their care. Sister Thecla was a woman of a noble type, strong, able, thoughtful, a great soul. It will be at once conceded, by those who knew them, that they who were sent to Memphis in 1873 were the flower of the Sisterhood of that day.

Scarcely had they commenced their work, when that terrible disease, the yellow-fever, appeared in Memphis. They immediately wrote to New York, and asked permission to remain at their posts and nurse the sick It was granted ; and so these three

* Miss Louise Caroline Darling, of Boston, Mass.

or four, of whom not one had had experience in epidemic disease, and whose special work was that of teaching, found themselves in the novel position of hospital sisters in a plague-stricken community. The summer passed; the fever ceased; and they resumed their proper work in the school, of which the opening had been postponed till late in the autumn of that year.

But worse things were to come. Five years later, as the summer of 1878 crept in with stealthy tread, there were rumours of a new visitation of the enemy; and in the month of August of that year, the yellow-fever was once more pronounced epidemic in Memphis. This time it came with tenfold force and fury.

Sister Constance and Sister Thecla were absent. At the closing of the School they had gone North, for greatly needed rest and change of air. On the 15th of August, the news reached them at St. Gabriel's, that Memphis was in confusion, and that thousands were flying from the place. This was two weeks only from the time of their arrival in New York: and without the loss of an hour their preparations were made, their farewells were said, and they were on the way back to Tennessee. A priest had hardly time to commit them to the mercy of God, when they were gone.

6

It was a striking contrast: on the one hand, crowds flying in terror, escaping by carriages, wagons, carts, and even on foot ; moody men, trembling women and children : on the other a few brave souls, with equal resolution, speeding into the valley of death; men of the medical profession, clergymen helping to assist the dying, hospital nurses, and the calm-faced daughters of the Lord seeking Him in His despairing people.

The little band on whom this storm burst consisted of the following persons :

The Rev. George C. Harris, D.D., Dean of St. Mary's Cathedral;

The Rev. Charles C. Parsons, Rector of Grace Church, Memphis;

Sister Constance, Superior;

Sister Thecla, teacher in St. Mary's School;

Sister Hughetta, teacher in St. Mary's School;

Sister Francis, in charge of the Church Orphan Home;

Mrs. C. Bullock and Miss Margaret Murdoch, both residents at the Sisters' House.

To these were subsequently added:

The Rev. Louis S. Schuyler;

The Rev. Wm. T. D. Dalzell;

Sister Ruth, and Sister Helen, sent from Trinity Hospital;

Sister Clare, of St. Margaret's, East Grinstead.

The Sisters' House was turned into a dispensary and store-house of supplies; the Orphan House was similarly utilized. At the request of the Relief Association, they also took charge of the " Canfield Asylum," on the 29th of August.

The work was incessant, like all work in time of violent epidemic disease. There were daily celebrations in the Cathedral; the blessed Sacrament was reserved, being constantly needed for the dying. In the narrative already referred to, many letters are given, pathetic, harrowing, terrible, descriptive of the scenes about them and the awful distress. Sister Constance kept a little diary, up to August 31st, when it ended. At that time Sister Thecla had been down but was better and at work again; 119 new cases had just been reported; and memoranda of death after death are strewn over the sad pages.

At last they sent to St. Gabriel's for some help. Mother Harriet would have gone long before, was eager to go, but was positively forbidden to take the risk; the General commanding is not the

proper person to lead the forlorn hope. Eager
volunteers besought permission to go; two were
selected, Sisters Ruth and Helen, whose training
at Trinity Hospital, as nurses of the sick in that
house, and in the worst places in the Fifth Ward
seemed to have fitted them for that honourable
service. Sister Ruth was in a retreat at St. Gabriel's when the summons came ; she left it at
once, and on the 31st of August, set off on her
journey, with Sister Helen and Sister Clare.
They arrived, Sept. 2d, and plunged at once into
the tide of that fatal flood.

On the 7th of September the Rev. Mr. Parsons
died ; the first to fall. Up to the time when he
became ill, the daily celebration was made in the
Cathedral. Dr. Harris was already down; they
had no priest; they were alone with God. When
this was known, many priests offered their services to the Bishop of Tennessee; of whom the
first to arrive was the Rev. Louis S. Schuyler, truly
an elect soul. It happened that he was at St.
Gabriel's holding a service, when the news of the
death of Mr. Parsons and the doubtful state of Dr.
Harris came: he learned it as he left the Chapel
early in the morning. On the 8th of September
he was in Memphis, arriving on the day after Dr.
Dalzell.

The end was now near for Sisters Constance and Thecla, who thus far had borne the heaviest burden. On the 7th they were both stricken and reported as very ill : that was the day on which Mr. Parsons died. A full account has been given of their passing.

Sister Constance died September 8th, Sister Thecla's only fear being that she might be stricken before her Sister's soul should have entered into rest.

On Thursday, the 12th, the brave soul of Sister Thecla departed.

On Saturday, the 14th, Dr. Armstrong, a faithful and beloved physician, died.

On Monday, the 16th, Mrs. Bullock died.

On Tuesday, the 17th, the Rev. Louis Schuyler died.

On the same day, a few hours later, Sister Ruth died.

On the 4th of October, after recovery and a relapse, Sister Frances died.

So the little band dwindled away.

On that 18th of September, they received, at Trinity Hospital, New York, this despatch:

" Sister Ruth entered into rest last night.
" *Beati mortui.*

" Only Sister Helen remains to be smitten of the fever.

" Sister Hughetta and Sister Clare are doing well."

It would be impossible, without long extracts from the letters of that period, to give an adequate idea of the beauty and dignity of those translations to the place beyond this vale of sorrow ; of Sister Thecla, suffering greatly, but patient through it all, her whole soul set on the Lord, chiding those about her who would have helped her in her agony, with the remonstrance, " I was with Jesus and you have disturbed me "; of the dear little Sister Ruth, beloved of all who knew her, dear to the children and poor in the New York slums, so quaintly mirthful, so bright, so cheery ; of Schuyler, and Parsons, brave men as ever lived; and finally, of Sister Constance, whose name, now after nearly twenty years, is a great power for devotion and righteousness wherever it is known.

She described with her own hand, soon to be relaxed in death, one of the last pictures seen by her in this world:

" Yesterday I found two young girls, who had spent two days in a two-room cottage, with the unburied bodies of their parents, their uncle in the utmost suffering and delirium, and no one near them but a rough negro drayman who held the sick man in his bed. It was twenty-four hours before I could get those two fearful corpses buried, and then I had to send for a police officer to the Board of Health before any undertaker would enter that room. One grows perfectly hardened to these things—carts with eight or nine corpses in rough boxes are ordinary sights. I saw a nurse stop one day and ask for a certain man's residence—the negro driver just pointed over his shoulder with his whip at the heap of coffins behind him and answered, ' I 've got him here in his coffin.' "

Sister Ruth, ere she followed her, gave some graphic sketches of her dear Superior's death. She spoke often of the children, the orphans ; sometimes she repeated Latin verses ; sometimes it was her accounts that disturbed her mind ; but in her delirium she was sweet and gentle, her voice always soft and low. She received the blessed Sacrament from Dr. Dalzell, who had just arrived to relieve the dead or dying priests: her eyes lit up. At the foot of the chalice were some white roses, almost the only ones then to be seen. At intervals she repeated the Ψ and $\mathbb{R}$, " O God, make speed to save us. O Lord make haste to help us." About midnight she cried aloud, " Hosanna " ; at 10 A.M. it was all over.

This is, in brief, the story of Memphis. It may be imagined how deep were the pain and anguish of those who, from a distance, looked on, unable to help save with their prayers. But in the record of the Community this is the page most brilliantly illuminated with the colours and the gold.

Were there a similar trial to be sustained to-day, no doubt the Sisters would embrace the occasion with the same enthusiasm : they know the value, the help, the moral and spiritual power flowing from such instances of devotion to the divine Master. As for the Southern Branch of the Community, they have felt, more deeply perhaps than it has been felt elsewhere, the benediction of that bitter baptism of suffering and pain: a very profound religious impression seems to give a peculiar tone to their work, a marked cast to their habit of mind. Those who fell on the field of duty may have been permitted to aid and strengthen others who never saw them, but to whom they were more a reality of the present than a memory of the past.

And now I shall add some words about a strange affair, which, if what we have been told is true, illustrates the power of a name and the force of an example. It is just to the Sisters to state that they have not desired that anything should be said outside on the subject, and that I proceed on my own responsibility, taking the risk of their disapproval. I refer to certain circumstances attending the death of a Sister who departed this life at Memphis, on the night immediately following Christmas Day, in 1887, after a distressing illness of a year's duration. There are several statements of what occurred, with some details which may be set down as fantastic, and unworthy of repetition ; but after carefully winnowing and sifting the mass, we come to the following particulars involving dates and matters of fact and not of fancy. It seems that during the month of November, in the year mentioned, this Sister had what she believed to be a revelation, made to her through Sister Constance, informing her of the precise date of her death, with minute specifications; that she related this at the time, and that her death did actually occur exactly as predicted. On or about the 15th of the month, after having received the Blessed Sacrament, she informed those present that she had seen Sister Constance in her room near her bed. Some days later she further stated, after a night of great suffering, that Sister Constance had come to her again, and sat beside her, and soothed her pain ; and that on being asked how

long she had to live, she was told, " Until Christmas." She then said to Sister Constance, " I
hoped to make my Communion on Christmas ";
and that Sister Constance replied, " You will do
so." Having further expressed a fear lest her
death might cast a cloud on the children's festivi-
ties she was told: " You will not die till late on
Christmas night, and before then you will be better, and suffer less, and the time will not seem
long."

They tried, it seems, to persuade Sister Isabelle
that this was a hallucination, and the effect of ex-
cited nerves; but she insisted that it was not a
dream, but had occurred precisely as she had
related it. And in that conviction she became
composed and calm, and so spent the time; and
everything turned out exactly as had been predicted. On Christmas Eve she was well enough
to sit up in her bed, and help to prepare the deco-
rations for the Cathedral, and dress dolls and fill
cornucopias for the children. On Christmas
morning she received the Sacrament with great
joy; soon after she became unconscious, and in
the ensuing night, at 2.20 A.M., she died.

That night a Sister dreamed that she saw an
angel standing over against the city who announced that he had come to bear away the soul

of Sister Isabelle; she awoke and said a prayer
for the dying, and looked at her watch, noting
the time as 20 minutes past 2. A little child who
was devoted to Sister Isabelle awoke her mother
in the night, exclaiming that she had seen in her
dream Sister Isabelle entering into Paradise.
One of the younger Associates, living in Constan-
tinople, dreamed that same night that she saw the
heavens opened and our Lord receiving Sister
Isabelle.

These are the particulars of that strange case.
Let each reader make of it what he will. It may
be set down as a psychological incident, or a
spiritual experience, or the result of imagination,
or a delusion. Members of the Community have
taken different views of the matter, as was to be
expected; we quarrel with no sceptic, and do not
insist on conformity with our own opinion. But
considering the nearness of the visible and invisible worlds, and what is included expressly or by
implication in the doctrine of the " Communion
of Saints "; considering that the Religious Life
where faithfully led, must act to loosen the bands
of the flesh, and open the eyes of the spirit; considering that there are things in heaven and earth
not dreamed of in our low and material philoso-
phies ; considering, to use the words of Keble,

that those "pure spirits" beyond may and do "soothe and haunt us night and day"; considering that God has often revealed things in dreams and visions, and that His angels are in close and intimate relations to the pilgrims of this night; we take leave to avow our belief in these and many like things, as having actually occurred, and are not ashamed to stand in the company of John Mason Neale,* Father Maturin, Frederick George Lee,† Wm. J. Knox Little,‡ and other firm believers in the Unseen World and in the possibility and likelihood of intercourse between the inhabitants of that world and us who are living here for a season.

The Reverend Mother was very much interested in this matter both as a psychological incident and a special experience ; but what her opinion about it was, she never told me, nor might it have been discreet to enquire too closely.

The Mother Superior never ceased lamenting

* "The Unseen World ; Communication with it, Real or Imaginary." By J. Mason Neale, D.D. 2d ed. Joseph Masters, London, 1853.

† "Glimpses of the Supernatural." By the Rev. Frederick George Lee. 2 vols. London, 1875.

‡ "The Broken Vow. A Story of Here and Hereafter." By W. J. Knox Little, Canon Residentiary of Worcester and Vicar of Hoar Cross, Staffordshire. 3d edition. London, Chapman & Hall, 1887.

the loss sustained by her and her children in the taking away of those noble and holy women. For years Sister Constance and the rest were an abiding memory, like the habit of a perpetually present sorrow. Again and again has the writer heard her lament, as one bereaved indeed, the loss of such daughters as those whom the Heavenly Bridegroom removed from sight for a while. The following summer was one of great anxiety lest the terrible scourge should be again inflicted on that unhappy place. A letter on that point, written in 1879, illustrates what all were dreading:

" I try not to think what the summer may be, only to be prepared, as far as may be, for whatever it shall please our Great High Priest to send us. Keep me informed of everything, which may seem to speak of the fever. I would not think it best for Sister E—— or Mrs. M—— to be exposed to it, if it is possible to save them from such exposure without injury to others. My own dear Sister, I understand so well what is in your heart when you say you can think of a long time of suffering with a wish to suffer. I should not dare to say it was presumption in your case. May our dear Lord give to you, and to me, what we most need for our sanctification: may we so yield ourselves to the operation of the Holy Ghost as in all things to be, and do, what He would have us be, and what He would have us do.

" With dearest love for all,

" Affectionately your Mother in our

" Blessed Lord."

VIII.

LETTERS.

M Y acquaintance with the Reverend Mother
began about the year 1865. She was one
of those persons who make an impression
which no lapse of time can efface. Probably she
owed to her remote French ancestors certain
striking characteristics in her bearing and actions;
her vivacity, her brightness, the conversational
charm which she possessed; her sympathetic interest in everything which came under her inspection. She had a very keen sense of humour, a
ready wit, and a merry laugh which was irresisti-
ble; she had the high-bred air distinctive of those
of gentle birth; a lady, all through. She reminded me of St. Theresa, as described by her
biographer, Cardinal Manning ; there were the
same simplicity of character, directness of purpose, activity of motion, humility of soul, self-
deprecation, which marked the Spanish woman;

94

indeed Mother Harriet, as I found out, had a
special admiration of Sister Theresa, and a great
love of her, and, no doubt, unconsciously, made
her a model in practice. She was a great worker,
and a great traveller, making long journeys from
point to point, visiting the Sisters, wherever scat-
tered abroad, and keeping herself informed of
everything relating to themselves, their lives, and
their respective houses in the East, the West, and
the South. As a business woman, she would
have taken a high place among men of that class;
thoroughly versed in whatever she needed to
know, wisely administering the financial affairs
of the Sisterhood, watchful, prudent, forecasting.
She had a heart full of sympathy for the troubles
of others; she shared the sorrows of each one of
her spiritual daughters; she was their confidant
and comforter. She suffered keenly whenever,
in that family of hers, anything went wrong;
when dissension troubled the domestic peace;
when tempers proved incompatible; when workers had to be changed from place to place; when
some lapsed and left their associates for alien
relations; when, as in some cases, unfortunate
women looked back, became discouraged, and
reverted to a world which they had renounced
with vows destined, alas! to be broken. Infinite

patience, unwearied love, unfailing pity were in
her soul; a strong desire for her own sanctification and that of all with whom she had to do.
As the slow years passed, bringing

"Many a sorrow, many a tear,"

one could see the furrowed lines of care deepening
on the features of her on whom that heavy load
was laid, but her bright, cheerful, hopeful spirit
never failed; within was calm and steadfast resolution; that well of delightful good humour still sent
forth its fresh and sparkling streams to gladden
and brighten the vale of misery; her trust in God
and her Beloved grew stronger, and the refrain of
the latter years was the ardent desire for the rest
of the Paradise of God.   Perhaps no one has ever
more fully illustrated in her life work, through all
its stages, these words, written in the breviary of
the Saint with whose spirit her own dwelt in such
harmony and affection:

> " Let nothing disturb thee,
> Let nothing affright thee.
> All passeth away,
> God only shall stay.
> Patience wins all.
> Who hath God needeth nothing,
> For God is his all."

Aet. 72.

An early Associate of the Sisterhood sent me some valuable and appreciative observations, drawn from her long and loving intimacy with the Mother, first as Sister Harriet, and then as the Superior, from which I make this extract:

" My own feeling is that the Mother's especial characteristic was the virtue of Hope, or perhaps I should say the Charity that ' hopeth all things.' Before I had ever seen her, and shortly after the foundation of the Sisterhood of St. Mary, I was told what struck me so forcibly that I have always remembered it; one of the Sisters had been talking about making a quest for money, and Sister Agnes said she thought it would be more important to seek candidates. Sister Harriet (as she was called then, indeed I believe I was one of the very first who called her Mother, before some of her own Sisters) answered that she always expected to go down to the door some morning, and see a whole row of women asking to be admitted into the Community. Certainly her prediction was fulfilled in a way she could hardly have imagined herself in those days of ' small things.'

" She was always very kind to me, from the time when I first knew her, through going to the Sheltering Arms to work for a little while. To manage the large tables full of children at meals was rather beyond my powers, and she came down so kindly to help me enforce discipline, and show the unruly children they would not be allowed to misbehave, tho' the one in charge was not a Sister.

7

"She was so fond, in later life, of the text
' Except a corn of wheat fall into the ground and
die, it abideth alone; but if it die, it bringeth
forth much fruit.' I have heard her dwell upon
that as a kind of epitome of what should be the
life of a religious community, in speaking of
various tribulations and trials through which their
own had had to pass. I think she felt sacrifice
to be the essential of the Religious Life, for the
individual and the Community so strongly."

The correspondence of the Reverend Mother
must have been immense. Her letters are carefully preserved in the houses of the Sisterhood as
sacred treasures. If these were accessible to the
general reader they would present that character
in the light in which it has been portrayed; but
that, of course, cannot be. A selection of them
has been most kindly sent to me for examination
and publication in this memoir.

"I found the selection difficult," says the Sister who sent them, "because the letters which
were most characteristic and telling, often had
personal references to individuals or situations
which made me shrink from sending them. I
have arranged the letters under subjects, hoping
to save trouble. The arrangement may not
always be obvious, but I think something may be
saved."

The arrangement shall be followed, in the transcription, although even these may have to be somewhat further pruned. They will be read with deeper interest, particularly by those younger members of the Community who knew the Mother less intimately, and by those who are to come after. These words of hers constitute a legacy to them, which will be reverently accepted and affectionately preserved. The reader will often find, in the preceding memoir, the explanation of matters referred to in the correspondence.

VOCATION.

" **St.** Mary's, Rockaway Beach,
" Aug. 14th.

" *My very dear Sister :*

" I received your letter on Tuesday of last week, and should have replied before, but for the coming here. Sister S—— returned on Wednesday evening, and I had many things to look after, that I might be free to leave on Thursday evening for New York. On Friday evening I came here; here at last, after the long waiting for a little rest and sea air. I should like to answer your letter in detail, but I know it is best for me just now not to write long letters. I am satisfied, nay I am more than that, I am sure that it is God's will that you should serve Him in the Religious Life, and that in His Providence you

were led to seek that life in this Community; and
I truly believe that as you surrender your whole
being more perfectly and entirely to the Divine
Will, so your vocation will become clearer to you
and you will marvel at the hesitation and the
holding back of the past. We may not look for
perfect unity of * opinion in a Community: there
must be diversity; it is impossible that all should
think alike on minor points, and even in graver
matters there will be differences. On general
principles there must be agreement. With a loving heart I say, my very dear Sister, come back
to us, and with us ' fight manfully unto your life's
end.'

" The Retreat will be somewhat shorter than
usual, for various reasons; it will begin with Vespers on Monday, Aug. 28th, and close on the
morning of Saturday, Sept. 2d. I should like
you to reach St. Gabriel's on Saturday, Aug.
26th. . . .

" I hope to have at least two weeks here for my
treatment, which consists in breathing the charming sea air and taking a few sea baths, and being
with forty or fifty children ; but I do not mind
their noise so long as I am not responsible for
them. I hope to take my first sea bath to night.
Sister —— is here and looking so well and
strong.

" With dearest love, believe me, ever most
affectionately yours in Xt,

" THE MOTHER."

* A blot appears on the sheet at the side, with this
explanation : " A mosquito caused this blot." No wonder, at Rockaway !

" St. Gabriel's, Peekskill,
" Dec. 14th.

" *My Dear Sister :*

" I think of you now as hard at work in the great city of Chicago (Sister F——'s pet). I imagine you will become greatly interested and absorbed in mission work; it is always fascinating and it is quite unlike your work of the past few years. I trust all will go well; but in every house we find trials awaiting us ; we must meet them, not in our own strength, but in the strength of the Great Master, who never fails us, if we leave all in His hands. You are now, as it were, making a new beginning. Dr. Pusey somewhere says, our whole life is one of new beginnings; and so it is, falling and rising again, time after time. . . . I think you know I cannot do much letter writing on account of my eyes, but you must write to me from time to time. My dear love to Sisters F—— and C——.

" Affectionately yours,
" THE MOTHER."

" St. Gabriel's School,
" Peekskill, N. Y.
" Oct. 28th, ——.

" *My dear Sister :*

" I am sure you are enjoying the old home faces and having a quiet time with your Sisters. I think of giving you to Sister Eleanor for a while to work in the Trinity Mission, but it is not fully settled yet. . . . We are filling up the vacant places in the Novitiate. Sisters M——

M—— and E—— P—— are in New York at St. Mary's Hospital ; in their places we have *four* ' minor postulants ' in the Choir: we have three, and soon will have four, Choir Postulants.   It is wonderful how God calls one after another to leave all and follow Him, and still the labourers are few.   We cannot begin to answer the calls upon us for work.''

MOTIVES TO WORK IN DEDICATED LIFE.

'' St. Gabriel's,
'' Peekskill,
'' Oct. 19th ——.

'' *My Dear Sister J——* :

'' Many thanks for your nice letter.   Do you know, it so happens that the month of September brought me, first your letter, then one from Sister L——, then one from Sister J——; and I hope to answer each one before the last day of October comes upon us, altho' I am not much up to letter writing; almost everything I try to do is done by a great effort.   .   .   .   Father Allen's sister has just died, and she is to be buried at Po'keepsie.   She once thought of coming to us.   No, dear Sister, it cannot matter what work we do, because we do all to the glory of God, and to Him.   Whether we offer the work of the hands, or the work of the intellect, it matters not.   We are living in a very wicked world, and judgment upon it cannot be far away.   Let us have our lamps trimmed, our ears alert to hear the voice of the Bridegroom, for He will surely come, He will not tarry.

"We have a very large household this year; the school is very full, and everybody is very busy. We have made a refectory of the little parlour, for the use of the School : if the Sisters had a house to go into, the School would soon turn us out of our present one. Thus far it does not seem to be God's will that we should begin our Convent, and I am content to do His will. With very dear love for you and all,

"Affectionately yours,
"THE MOTHER."

"St. Gabriel's, Nov. 13, 1891.

"*My dearest Sister:*

"Yes: it is some time since I have written to you, but I know you will forgive me. I have been so pressed at every turn, and my eye is very weak, and I am often obliged to stop in the midst of my writing and give that one eye a rest. It does not pain me in the least but is very, very weak. I spent two weeks at ——, and on my return found such a load of work! I was days and days getting at the bottom of it. . . . I will not write of all that is in my mind concerning the action of the Society.* The Church is certainly passing through a great crisis, and I may say, Religious Orders through a still greater crisis than even the Church. I feel like one who is holding on to some tender, small tree, the tree looking as if there was scarcely anything to hold on to, yet feeling sure that the root, which one could not see, was firm, strong, solid, and would not fail

* The reference is to the Evangelist Fathers.

one. . . . The lesson of detachment is a very
hard lesson for most of us to learn. . . . I
hope the points of the Chapter * would have been
sent before this. . . . The point about the
Offices was not one of my points. I suppose the
idea in the minds of the Sisters was, that it was
an occasional thing happening seldom. I should
be very sorry to have the memorials left out, except now and then in case of necessity. Are you
quite sure that the Offices must be so said ? I
fancied, with school work, Sext and Nones could
be managed separately for the most part. . . .
My special love to dear Sister H. T—— and to
all. I am having many worries just now; if one
had only some one to look to for help! but such is
not God's will, and there must be perfect trust
and no murmuring."

ACCEPTANCE OF THE WILL OF GOD.

" Feby. 25th.

" Dearest Sister :

" Your letter of yesterday was very discouraging. I shall anxiously await the word of the
Chicago doctor. I understand the ' I think.' I
cannot feel that dearest Sister will not get better,
yet I fear. May we all accept lovingly whatever
God has in store for us concerning our beloved.
It pleased Him to take my first Sister Constance;
if it is His will to take my second Sister Constance

---

* Prior to the meetings in Chapter, a list of topics to be
considered appears to have been sent to each one entitled
to a place and a vote.

it must be right. Give love to the precious in-
valid from us all: we pray constantly for her, **and**
also for our dear Sister A——.

"I trust you will have that supernatural
strength given you which you need, for only the
supernatural can help you to bear all cheerfully.

"Ever lovingly in our Blessed Lord,
"THE MOTHER."

"St. Gabriel's,
"June 3, 1884.

"*My very dear Sister:*

"I am good for nothing to-day, not feeling at
all well, but I must manage to answer your letter.
. . . I always say, if there exists the need,
and one has counted the cost as in the sight of
God, one must undoubtedly make the venture of
faith, believing that 'the Lord will provide'; it
would be difficult for me to express in words how
very strong that feeling is with me. . . .
Our little addition gives us a nice class-room, and
six alcoves, each containing an entire window.
This, including the fitting up of the alcoves, putting in gas pipes, etc., etc., cost $1200, and it has
been paid from the school receipts of the year. I
suppose you will use brick .* Not having that
interest to pay gives a chance of meeting expenses. I hope the Trustees will not borrow
money to pay it and so increase the debt. I cannot remember telling you that the first few years
the interest was all at 8 and 10 per cent. You
can imagine the drain on the School fund: I was

* The reference is to work at Kenosha.

amazed; it seemed like usury to me.   I think now
it is all reduced to 6 pr. ct.   .   .   .   You will
have to be wonderfully busy to get ready for the
Retreat in the short interim of School closing and
Retreat beginning.   You are fortunate in having
Father Maturin again.   We shall remember the
Mission."

"St. Gabriel's, Sept. 7, 1885.

"Dearest Sister :

" I take it for granted the telegram was recd.
and that our dear Sister is by this time safely at
St. Paul's: the change will be good for her in addition to the medical advice.   .   .   .   The day
for the Profession is not yet determined upon: I
will write as soon as I know, if only a postal.
.   .   .   I feel greatly distressed when I realize
how I have failed to rise up to the difficulties of
the past year, which certainly have been great,
yet their greatness is no excuse for my spiritual
weakness nor do I know that I ought to excuse
anything on account of physical weakness, yet
that too has been very great.   I wonder sometimes how it came about that I should be so nervously unstrung: that is passing off and we will
hope that it will soon be all gone."

The following letter refers to a visit to a Sisterhood which had been established in Toronto, in
the Dominion of Canada.   The Sisters of St.
Mary felt a great interest in it, for the reason

that the founders were trained in New York, so
that it was, as it were, a mission offshoot of their
own Community. Mother Harriet speaks of it
in a letter written at St. Gabriel's, as follows:

" We had two Novices admitted this morning:
one is for the Canada Sisterhood. I think you
know we are training two Canadians to be returned to Toronto, to found there a Sisterhood.
Sister Hannah, who is to be the Superior, will
probably be professed in September and go directly to Toronto. Sister Hannah goes to New
York this week to get a little insight into our
work in the city; you may see her at the Infirmary, Varick St. It has been very pleasant to have
the training of these two Sisters : one would
hardly have thought that St. Mary's would have
trained two *Englishwomen* for the Religious Life.
' God moves in a mysterious way, His wonders to
perform.' "

" St. Gabriel's, Peekskill,
" April 21, 1886.

" *My very dear Sister :*

" You will think me long in writing, but the
days are so full just now. I reached Toronto in
good time, without mishap of any sort or kind. I
found no one awaiting me ; my letter did not
reach Mother Hannah in time; but I easily obtained a carriage and was soon at my destination.
I had a very charming visit, all were so kind. I
had two drives, seeing all that was worth seeing

of Toronto. The Sisters are very pleasantly situated, and are getting on nicely in every way. At present, the novitiate consists of three Novices and three Postulants. Nursing is quite a feature of their work. I left Toronto at 3.55 on Saturday afternoon, and was obliged to change cars three times before reaching Peekskill, at which place I arrived safely on Sunday morning at 10 o'clk. I found Sister F—— very ill; congestion of the lungs; one of the maids also very ill with lung trouble; this morning she passed away into that other world; she was one of our own people, and not a Romanist; we are glad about that. She will be buried from here, probably on Saturday. She was a good girl; she was able to receive the Blessed Sacrament yesterday morning. Sister Agnes is not so well; there can be no thought of her going far from home: I begin to fear that she may not rally from this illness. Sister S—— or myself will go down to see her directly after Easter. I feel as if the next autumn would bring with it great difficulties, but I know that whatever comes, all is from a loving God, and I trust we may all be guided and strengthened to meet whatever trials may be in store for us. I thought so constantly of you, dear Sister, after our parting at the station; the returning alone to Kemper Hall; but I am so sure you are able to bear this sorrow, to accept lovingly God's will for you. May we not believe that the spirit of our sweet Sister will hover over the house, and that you and all will feel the nearness? With dearest love for you and all,

"Lovingly,

"THE MOTHER."

"St. Gabriel's, March 28, 1888.

"*My very dear Sister:*

"I must write **you** a line to-day because it is March 28th, and we remember that two years ago the soul of our sweet Sister passed away, entering into that life eternal, that new life that knows no ending. To-day it is Wednesday; that other day it was Sunday, the Lord's Day ; so fitting for our dear Sister to go to Him on His own Day.*

"I received your note about the change of quarters in Chicago. I do so want to see the Chicago home! Our Novitiate has not had as many recruits this last year: I dare say it will soon take a fresh start again soon. I have several letters just now about candidates.

"With dearest Easter love for all,

"Affectionately yours.

"St. Gabriel's, Nov. 11, 1890.

"*My very dear Sister:*

"I am afraid you will **think** I have quite forgotten you, it is so long since I have written: dearest Sister, believe me, I do **not** forget you even for a moment, nor do I forget the little points you ask me about. I have a little box and drop into it the queries from time to time as I receive them. I have been so very, very busy, and I have not always felt up to letter writing, when

---

* It will be remembered that the **Mother herself had** the honour of being taken on **Easter Day.**

the writing could be postponed. You can hardly think how I *long* for Kemper Hall to be *almost* the very same as the Mother House.* God in His wisdom took from it our precious Sister E—— who seemed so necessary from our point of view; now He may will to take Sister H—— T——, and if we could have our way, how we would have both with us, would we not ? Yet we know without a shadow of doubt that all things work together for good. Sister E——'s *balancing power* was something wonderful, still God willed that the work was to go on without her."

CURRENT EVENTS IN THE CHURCH.

Alluding to the defection of Father Rivington, one of the Society of St. John the Evangelist, she writes:

" St. Mary's, 8 E. 46th St.
" April 13th,

" I have before me your letter of woes. I mean, however, to look on the bright side of it just now. I say to myself : I would rather hear that one of my dear Sisters had entered Paradise, than to hear she had left the Church of her baptism for the Church of Rome. I mean, any Sister of mind and position. I do not, of course, mean just any Sister, whose mental powers one could not hold

* This seems to be a reference to her wish for a kind of provincial arrangement of the branches in the South and West.

in esteem. Father Rivington's action passes my comprehension."

She made several visits to England. Previous to one of these she writes :

" I wish very much to go to England this spring, and study up a few points concerning religious Orders: if any kind Associate will give us a little money I can manage it, but we cannot afford the expense. I should take Sister C—— with me. But alas! for the filthy lucre! where is it to come from ? "

"St. Gabriel's, Peekskill,
"Nov. 14, 1883.

" *My very dear Sister :*

" I have your nice, long letter; also the little note telling me of the case of fever, which I hope most earnestly is not a very serious one. Thus far we have gotten on without much illness, a few little ailments only.

" I did not enter much into the Prayer Book matters as handled at the Convention; I hardly know what was proposed. . . . You know all about the translation of our dear Dr. Ewer; I was one of his admirers. Have you heard of the death of our sweet Lily D——? only twelve hours' illness, and her pure spirit departed : the idol of the family and loved by all who knew her. I grieve for her dear mother and father; the latter seems utterly crushed. . . . As you see, I am

' Monarch of all I survey,' Community, Novitiate, Housekeeping, etc., etc. We are making
additional refectory room for the children. We
have a young girl with us as candidate for the
Minors; I hope she will remain and go on.''

ANNIVERSARIES OF PROFESSIONS.

'' Jany. 25, 1887.

'' Just a word of love on this your day. I am
reminded of the poem, ' We are Seven.' Our
seventh is at rest, the six still toiling on in this
lower world, doing His will most imperfectly,
while our seventh, may we not believe, thinks
of us, joins her prayers with ours, as she does that
will more perfectly in her Paradise of Rest in the
Heavenly Home. The day is very beautiful here,
and the two of the seven here are unusually well
and bright. . . . On Thursday, if all is well,
I propose to start for Memphis—Sister H—— is
to go with me. I feel that I must give all the
time I have to spare from here to Memphis, and
I ought to be back by the end of March, I hope
before the 28th. This year that day falls in Passion Week.''

'' ——, —, 1888.

'' This is your day with all its beautiful lessons
and all its memories of joy and sadness. I can
scarcely realize so many years have passed since
that Profession Day. . . . Our day is almost
here ; we shall probably have the usual Chapter
on the Octave of the Purification.''

VACATIONS FOR SISTERS.

It seems to have been a part of the duty of the Reverend Mother to plan the vacations so that the workers might be relieved and the work go on. Many letters are taken up with these arrangements, involving much thought and consideration.

" I sent the telegram : I am quite clear that Sister F—— should go to her mother at this juncture: as to who shall be sent to Chicago, I am uncertain."

" I sent the night telegram begging you to set off to Clifton as soon as possible. Your letter was delayed again, being sent to that unknown place that once before took one of your letters about dear Sister. I am glad the Retreat was so fully attended and appreciated. How wonderful are God's ways! And how much He permits us, poor weak mortals, to do for Him!"

" St. Mary's, Rockaway.

" I am just sending a telegram saying, by all means take the California trip. I am more than delighted at the proposal for you, it quite seems to cover the whole ground. Don't say, three weeks; say, four, five, yes, even six! Now as to crossing the sea another year : who can tell what may happen before another year comes round?

Do plan everything *new* without reference to that. I beg you will take full time and over. I know that the Sisters and Teachers will all be faithfulness itself, and it is so important that you have a change, absolute change and rest; important for you, and important for those working under you. We go to the city to-day. We have had two storms for my benefit (I love a high sea) and the two yachts passed us for our benefit also; so I had a full view of the great race of the season. I am writing in great haste, as everything must be packed away this morning.''

" St. Gabriel's.

" I am just leaving here for N. Y. on Hospital business which seems to have neither beginning nor end; it obliges me also to go to White Plains, and I am stealing a little time to write to you before I leave. . . . Sister J——'s aunt has secured a promise from us that she should pay her a visit: she will go directly her aunt returns, and then we will forward her to you. . . . Your month off, now: nothing must prevent you from going away for one full month, and leaving all your cares behind you. The Sisters are perfectly capable of going on, and you must, as I say, have a full month; we will not put it four weeks, but one full month. You know, dear Sister, I am not an Autocrat, but you may call me such in this matter or give me any bad name you like, and I'll not say a word. As for the expenses, that is not to be mentioned; you are entitled to whatever you need, and you must be sure to do that which will be the most perfect rest to you. And now I have got to the end of my paper.''

" St. Gabriel's, July 31, 1894.

" We shall be delighted to see you and Sister
F—— once more, and have you with us for the
Retreat, which begins with the Vespers of Mon-
day, Aug. 27th, and closes with the celebration on
Saturday, Sept. 1st. We could not take in a
Sunday, as Father Benson was obliged to be in
Boston for Sunday duty. I see no objection to
your stopping over to consult the Doctor. . . .
Oh, this heat! I am almost melting: it seems
sometimes as if I could not endure another day,
and vegetation is crying piteously for a little rain;
a little rain, but the little rain don't come."

ENJOYMENT OF OFFICES.

" St. Thomas' Day,
" *O Rex Gentium.*

" This is St. Thomas' Day, and we are reminded that the Great Feast is very near. How
beautiful the ' Great O's ' are, as day by day we
approach the Feast! * To say the Divine Office

* Some of our readers may need to be informed that by
the " Great O's " are meant the Antiphons to the Mag-
nificat sung during the third and fourth weeks of Advent ;
they were as follows :

Dec. 16th, *O Sapientia.*
"   17th, *O Adonai.*
"   18th, *O Radix Jesse.*
"   19th, *O Clavis David.*
"   20th, *O Oriens.*
"   22d, *O Rex Gentium.*
"   23d, *O Emmanuel.*

is indeed one of the great joys of the Religious
Life: I love it more and more, although I have
been compelled to give up Matins since that illness of mine."

"St. Gabriel's, April 10, 1884.

"*My dear Sister:*

"It is Maundy Thursday: our Matins and
Lauds for this day, may I say it? were *perfect.* I
think the Office was never more beautifully ren-
dered in our Chapel than last night at 12. Oh!
what a mystery this week is! Shall we understand it all some day? With dearest love for all,
ever lovingly yours, in the Crucified One."

"St. Gabriel's, Dec. 27, 1890.

"*My dear Sister:*

"I sent off a hasty scrap yesterday: now I will
write not so hastily.

"We say the Peace of the Church on Advent
Ember Days. There is no regulation as to abstinence when travelling; a matter of that kind
must be governed by circumstances; it might be
best at one time, and not at all best at another
time. Whenever Sext and Nones are said together it should be by aggregation: there should
be no provision for any other way for saying the
two Offices together. . . . We had our usual
Christmas Offices; we began Matins at 10.45 and
went on until 2. I was well tired when I went
to my room, and not equal to rising at 6 A.M.
All these years I have been able to have the mid-

night services at Christmas and again in Holy
Week. I wonder if I shall have many more.
Tears are passing ; the time cannot be far off,
when mine will no more be passing, but past. I
send you a motto for the coming year.* I hope
the sky will be a little clearer for you, dear Sister,
as the days go by. We know our discipline comes
from God, and we must vindicate God by our acceptance of it. Have you read Godet's Studies
on the Old Testament ? If not, try to get the
book and read his exposition of Job. With dear
love, affectionately yours,

" THE MOTHER."

In another letter, which I have mislaid, she
wrote to this effect: " The longer I live the more
I delight in the study of the Bible: I am becoming a *Bible Christian*."

ILLNESS AND DEATH AMONG THE SISTERS.

Of the letters entrusted to my care, none are
more touching than those written on occasion of
fatal illness and impending death in the Community, or after the departure of some elect soul to
the rest of Paradise. From these I hesitate to
make many extracts : they might sadden and de-
press the reader, or appear like violations of the

---

* The motto was, "Thy Will, Thy blessed Will, whatever it may be."

sanctity of sorrow. But in them all comes out
the loving tenderness of the Mother's heart, and
they show how habitual was the thought of the
vanity of life and the near approach of the end.
Words of comfort and consolation abound; sooth-
ing, tender words, which none knew better how
to speak to the mourning heart. Some brief extracts will suffice, taken here and there from a
large number now before my eye. The following
contains an impressive description of a Christian
transit hence.

"Kemper Hall, Kenosha, Wis.,
"March 29, 1886.

"*My Dear Sister:*

"Our dear little Sister Elise passed away at
the hour of Prime on Sunday morning, the first
hour (ecclesiastical) of the Resurrection Day, and
on the 28th of the month (four times seven). All
through the day before she was very weak, and it
seemed as if she could not survive the night;
none of us went to bed. About twelve I went to
my room, lying down dressed, thinking any moment I might be called; but I was not called till
I was preparing to go down to Prime. We were
all with her. I read the short office from our
Manual for the dying : then we all repeated the
Creed and the Lord's Prayer. She ceased to
breathe so quietly that we hardly knew the exact
moment ; but Sister M—— C—— took out her
watch, and it was precisely half past six. We

then said the office in our Manual for one departed; lingered a few moments; then went down
to Chapel and said Prime without ringing the
Chapel bell. The funeral service will be in the
Chapel to-morrow morning : there will be two
celebrations. I think I never knew a more quiet
departure or more quiet illness. Everything in
regard to the School went on as usual; no noise
disturbed Sister, and she wished everything to go
on up to the last moment. A characteristic illness and death in her case, just as it was in Sister
Esther's : and now we have another name to add
to our March commemorations. Sister made her
last Communion on Saturday at 12 noon."

In this letter I find a slip of paper written in
another hand; that of a priest who was there at
the time.

" Praise to God for the deliverance of Sr. Elise,
a very sweet, true, pure soul, perfected through
suffering and fit for Paradise."

Sister Agnes will long be remembered as the
accomplished and admirable head of St. Mary's
School in 46th St.; a wonderful woman, for the
perfect calmness, quietness, and steadiness of her
ways, and her great influence on all who came in
contact with her ; nothing ever seemed to ruffle,
disquiet, or trouble her.

The Reverend Mother, in a letter written at St.
Gabriel's, Nov. 4th, refers to her illness.

" Sister Agnes is, I think, slowly but surely passing away. She still clings to the daily routine. I hope to see her soon, but I cannot be much away in Sister ——'s absence. . . . We did not have a ceremonial procession to the Cemetery on All Souls' Day, but we all visited it, and laid our gifts of flowers and bright leaves on the graves of our beloved ones. The day was perfect.''

In another letter she gives some particulars of the transit of that brave, calm, earnest woman.

" St. Mary's, E. 46th St.
" April 28th.

" Our dear Sister Agnes entered into rest on Thursday, April 21st, at 10.15 A.M. She suffered very much all through her illness, and the last two days from great restlessness. . . . Sister was in the Community room, dressed as usual, on Tuesday morning, but at noon she said she felt so very ill she must go to bed. From that time she failed; and on Saturday we laid her to rest in our quiet Cemetery. Dr. Richey went up with us, as well as Dr. Houghton. All the funeral service was private. As we left the Cemetery a little robin on the top of a tree began singing with all his might. Dr. Houghton says, ' Who that was present can ever forget that song ? ' ''

A few more notes may be added to these pathetic descriptions, taken here and there from the papers before me.

" April 29, 1891.

" I had a faint hope that our sweet little Sister **Helen** Theodora might rally with the warm weather, and possibly might be **able** to come home, and so finally rest with us **here.** But **your** letter makes it clear that this cannot **be**: give **her** my dearest, sweetest love, and tell **her** I had so hoped **to** see her once more. As **I** go into the Mortuary Chapel from time **to time I** often say to myself, who of **us** will first **find rest** here? We have many delicate Sisters, now ; very **many**; yet it may be that **the** strongest and least **ailing** will **be the** first called."

" **I** am reading with *intense* interest **the ' Mys-** tery of Pain " ; I brought it with **me from Mem-** phis."

" The weather is very hard upon me [written **in** August during great heat], and there is so much to do and so much to think about. The telegram telling us of the death of the All Saints' Superior read ' Our Reverend Mother Rests.' That **one** word, ' rests,' how much is contained in it !"

" Dec. 22d.

" Before this reaches you, you will have entered into the Christmas joy, have taken the Christ Child afresh into your heart. May all Christmas joys be with you, and all the dear Sisters with you. I am thinking so much of our sweet Sis- ter ——, as this precious season draws near. Before determining the time of Sister S——'s visit, I would like to know as nearly as possible just how she is. I wish above all things that Sister S—— might be with her when those last hours seem to be very near: please write me how it is."

"Jany. 12, 1888.

".   .   .   .   You have received before this the news of Miss M——'s death. Sisters, Postulants, Associates, one after the other, and pupils too ; all passing through the gate of death, all entering into the Blessed Presence. Miss M—— was ready for the change. Mary Parker we shall miss sorely ; she had given herself to God, and the offering was accepted." *

"Feby. 6th.

".   .   .   .   A thousand thanks to you and all the dear Sisters for their loving remembrances. I steal a little time in the midst of ' *our week* ' † to write a few words for you all and to tell you that right in the midst of ' our week ' we say our last words over dear Sister Gabrielle. To-day we lay her away in her lonely bed: now she is in the Chapel, and her face is very sweet, and beautiful,

* A memorial window bearing the name of this lovely young girl may be seen in the Trinity Mission House, No. 211 Fulton St. She was the only daughter of the Rev. Dr. Stevens Parker ; as pure a soul as ever passed hence into the light beyond.

† The reference is to the anniversary of the Community, and the Chapter then held each year.

and peaceful. . . . She never lost her consciousness for one moment. She was only 22. In the midst of life we are in death."

Referring to the death of another Sister and her burial at St. Gabriel's, she writes:

" She was one of the seven at your profession: she came between you and Sister F——. Sister Eleanor went on to her and reached Augusta in time to be with her several hours. She especially asked to be taken to Peekskill for burial ; it seemed to have been much on her mind. Now, the Seven are divided ; five in the Church Militant, two in the Church Triumphant; and so, one by one, we go on our lonely journey, as one by one we entered into this world. . . . One by one we drop out and another takes our place; and so it will go on and on until that Second Coming. " Have you seen the book, ' Earth's Earliest Ages ' ? The author seems to think the world now is much as it was in the days of Noah ; touches upon the Theosophy of the present day, etc., etc. Well, we know God rules over all, while apparently Satan is having it all in his own way; this Theosophy is certainly a special device of his to ruin souls."

SCHOOL SUPERVISION.

The charge of four large schools, with constant attention, not only to the expenditures and re-

ceipts, but also to the details of the management
of those institutions, one in the City of New York,
another in Putnam County, a third in Wisconsin,
and a fourth in Tennessee, must have been most
exacting and laborious. Allusions to the school
work are constant. A postcript to a letter written at Rockaway Beach says:

" K. H. has 64.
" St. G.'s 54; last year we managed to stow
away 58; this year all are large girls; we can
only manage for 54."

Of Kemper Hall she writes:

" Sister F—— seems wonderfully well again; I
hope she may continue so; I am surprised to see
how much she seems able to do. I think she has
all her classes except Astronomy; she could not
go to the Observatory, so Miss H—— has that
class."

Kemper Hall stands on Lake Michigan: there
was when the Sisters first took charge of it a great
deal of trouble, with heavy expenses, in protect-
ing the front by a breakwater or dyke from the
heavy waves on the shore.

" Thanks for your note, and the account of the

fearful storm. At the rate of 15 ft. a storm, how soon would the house go ? Can you do that sum ? I received a letter from the Bishop about some definite plan for the School, but I could not say anything about it until we could talk it all over; and besides I have a fancy for Dr. —— seeing the property; you know he could easily manage this at the time of the General Convention.* . . . I have just heard of the death of Dr. Mulford: I think you knew he was a friend of mine. He was only 51 in years, and we thought him strong in body as well as strong in mind, and he was altogether a most charming man : *you* would have enjoyed him thoroughly, had you known him. As a scholar he was wonderful. I shall cherish his last gift to me, ' The Republic of God.' ''

One who was very intimate with her writes as follows:

" Ever since I have known the Mother I have found her interested in every branch of Natural Science, especially, of late, in the subject of light and recent discoveries in that department of knowledge. She was glad to discuss these subjects with others and eager to interest them in the same. It was her habit to reserve articles which specially pleased her, for the girls in the School. Just before her departure she had been reading Canon McColl's ' Life Here and Here-

* Held in Chicago, in 1886.

after,' a book on ' Our Life after Death,' and Willink's ' World of the Unseen.' "

A LIGHT AND A SHADOW.

" St. Mary's, Memphis,
" Tenn.
" February 11th.

" TO THE REV. W. C. F——., D.D.

Rev. and Dear Sir :

" It gives us all great pleasure to receive your beloved daughter, and the more so because of your tender letter of commendation.

" I trust God has indeed chosen her to be among His special ones; the elect of the chosen, if one may so express it; that is, if we may, while we call the whole body of the Church the Elect, call all Religious Orders within the Church, the elect of the elect.

" I left St. Gabriel's on the evening of Thursday the 3d, and will probably not be home again until the end of March.

" I passed through Cleveland on Friday, and thought of you and yours, as the train stopped for a few minutes at the depot.

" With true regards, believe me,
" Sincerely and reverently yours,
" ✠ HARRIET,
" Mr. Supr. Com. S. M."

(Copied by Mrs. F——).

" Trinity Hospital,
" Nov. 9th.

" *My dear Sister :*

" Will you kindly tell the Sisters with you that Sister M—— E—— has left the Community and intends joining the Roman Church. I need not add, that this is a trial to us all, but we will forgive her the wrong, and try to forget it, saying as little as possible of what she has done.

" Affectionately,
" THE MOTHER."

IX.

THE PASSING.

THE voices of Nature speak directly to the ear of man. None, perhaps, are more expressive than those heard towards the declining of the day by one who, having still with him in the body some dearly beloved and venerated friend, or more than friend, reads in the sunset skies the presage of parting. The day going away, the shadows of the evening stretching out, the golden glory flaming in the west announce the nearness of the end; near as is the end of the day, so near is the end of life; and, with a sudden anguish and a grip at the heart which only they can comprehend who have felt it, men realize the pain of separation, the shortness of the time, and the nearness of the hour when other words will cease in that last word, farewell.

Step by step we have followed one in her earthly pilgrimage : it remains only to muse of the time and the manner of her passage from this scene.

Notwithstanding the prevailing tone of cheerfulness in her letters, there is reason to believe that the last two years were full of anxiety and trouble. Perhaps this was to be expected, considering the wonderful growth of the Sisterhood, the intricacies of its business and work, the occasional clashing of interests, the proceedings of some thoughtless and difficult members, the mishaps and misadventures encountered in every large society, and the advancing age and declining powers of its head. It is a rule of the Sisterhood that the Superior shall be re-elected after an interval of three years. For several terms, the Mother was thus re-elected until at length the formality was omitted through the wish and intention of her companions that she should continue in office all her life. Notwithstanding she often expressed the conviction that it might be better for her to withdraw, and to seek time for undisturbed preparation for her change: that wish was overruled by the Chapter, and for her the day of rest was put off until she was taken to it in Christ through the portal of the grave.

In the spring of 1894, the Mother made her last visit to the South. A letter from a Sister

9

now at Memphis gives a pleasant account of the
visit.

"During her stay with us we celebrated the
70th anniversary of her birth. She was as delighted as a child with everything done for her
pleasure. On the morning of her birthday the
School children brought her a large silver tray of
roses. 'There must be fifty roses here!' she
exclaimed on receiving them.

" 'There are just seventy,' the little children
replied, and Mother was delighted. On the evening of the same day the Academic Classes entertained the Mother with an excellent rendering
of 'The Merchant of Venice.' She was full of
enthusiasm over the play, declaring to the great
amusement of the students, that she herself could
not have done the part of the Jew half so well.
To which one of the children replied, 'We did
not suppose, Mother, that you could have done
the *Jew's* part at all.' At this the Mother laughed
heartily.

"As Superior General of 'The Guild of the
Holy Child Jesus,' she took great pleasure in the
work of the Southern Branch of the Guild. We
always arranged to have a reception of new members into the Guild at the time of her visits.
Once while viewing the long procession of beautiful white-veiled children returning from the
Cathedral to the School after their joyful musical
service, she expressed her pleasure, commenting
upon some special features of the service. It is
the custom with us for the children received into
the Guild to wear wreaths of white roses as a dis-

tinction from the other members ; and for two children to accompany the Cross-bearer carrying slender banners of white satin and gold bearing the words ' JESU King of kings ' and ' JESU LORD of lords.'   Mother was delighted with all and said to me, ' How little did Sister E——, Sister M—— M—— and I think that the little Guild we organized in 1869 would grow to be anything so beautiful and good as this ! '

'' Mother was always lovingly interested in our Orphanage. '' These dear little children,'' she would say, '' have no one but us to look to: how faithful we should be to our trust! ''

Great indeed was her love for children and deep the interest she took in them.   Here and there instances of this come back to us.   There was a young child whose birthday was the same as that of the Reverend Mother, the 7th of May.   On the child's eighth birthday, she received a letter from the Mother alluding to the coincidence and saying, '' You are now 8, and I am 8 times 8.'' Thenceforth they always kept their birthdays together, exchanging loving greetings, till 8 more years had passed, when the child of 16 and the holy woman of 72 sent their last messages to each other.   From the Sisters was sent to the child the copy of the *De Imitatione*, well worn by long use, which the Mother kept in her stall in the Chapel at St. Gabriel's : a treasure worth more than any earthly price to an appreciative and loving heart.

In confirmation of the impression that the last years brought some special trials, the following letters demand insertion:

"Jany. 31, 1895.

". . . . I am sorry Sister F—— is so out of health, but God knows best and we can only accept His will in all things. We mourned for our dear Sister Paula, but we know that to depart and be with Christ is far better ; and she is safe ; the turmoil is all over and the rest has come."

"Sept. 13, 1895.

" I have had rather a trying summer in many ways, but, as you know, I do not lose heart. I *know* and am *sure*, that all is from God, and that His very chastisements are tokens of His love. The grace of humility cannot be ours, unless we have humiliations. I try to obey that clause in our Rule * which says: ' Be thankful for humiliation of whatever kind.' "

"St. John's Day, 1895.

". . . . Dear Sister, you have not been cross with me : I cannot write or even speak of the past year. I have suffered too deeply. ' Yea,

---

* The Inner Rule must be the one referred to.

a sword shall pierce through thine own soul also. If our patron saint is the ' Mater Dolorosa,' our tears must blend with hers. I wonder sometimes whether I shall ever go West and South again. I have entered upon my 73d year and must soon be laid aside. I would like to have a little quiet time ' before I go hence and be no more seen.' ''

Date wanting.

" I know you are very weary and things look rather dark; but as a matter of fact things are not really dark. God ruleth over all, and if we feel troubled, is it not a want of faith on our part ? Just think of our blessings : what are our trials compared to our blessings ? . . . I realize that the checks we receive as a Community are blessings in disguise. Sometimes it comes to me we are too worldly, do too much to please people outside ; so let us believe that when God speaks to us as He has in the events of the past summer, that He longs to make us all more entirely His own, that He would have our very best. . . . I am writing you a long letter, and have still something more to say: when the School is fairly in order, you must go away for a rest. This is a positive command; do not think it cannot be."

Up to the very last she was actively engaged in the duties of her position, as actively, at least, as growing infirmities would permit. It was a great happiness to her that she lived to see the completion of the Chapel at St. Gabriel's. She insisted that there should be no molestful begging for it; no canvassing for contributions even among the Associates; she wished it to be as nearly as possible a free-will gift and offering of love. The Mother made many quiet suggestions, in that mirthful spirit so characteristic of her, about the Chapel. In England nothing struck her so much as Durham Cathedral, and she declared that it was her desire and intention that the Chapel should be built on the model of Durham. It is not quite so large, nor is it calculated to remind the visitor of that structure; but it is a very beautiful Chapel, and when she saw it finished she might well have sung her Nunc Dimittis.

The last official act of Mother Harriet was a visit to St. Mary's Hospital in New York, made some three weeks before her death, in order to complete the arrangements for the establishment of a Summer Home for Children at Norwalk, Conn. In 1881, through the kindness of a friend, land was purchased at Rockaway Beach, and a Seaside Home was erected there. The Reverend Mother was passionately fond of the ocean; for some years her only recreation consisted of a few days, now and then, at Rockaway; some of the letters already transcribed for this memoir were written there; but she realized the fact that it

St. Mary's Chapel, Peekskill.

was better to abandon the place, in consequence of its growing disadvantages and inconveniences, and gladly consented to the transfer of that branch of the work to a new site. A lady of this city, widely known throughout the land for her gracious acts of benevolence, gave the Sisters 31 acres of land, and $20,000, for a building to be erected at Norwalk, a property once owned by the Cannon family, and associated in Mother Harriet's thoughts with recollections of her early days. The Home will accommodate some seventy children, and the buildings will soon be begun. It is pleasant to reflect that as her ministrations of mercy began among the children, so they ended in the same tender companionship with those lambs of the flock of Christ, that Great Shepherd of the sheep.

In the life of St. Theresa we read that, at the last, her one thought was, "After all, I am a child of the Church"; and in that fact she stayed her hope and trust in the mercy of the Lord. Our dear Mother had a spirit as humble and reverent as that of her great exemplar, but she also had an almost exultant trust, a hopeful assurance, of the power and love which never had failed her, and in which she was joyful and glad. In her allusions to her approaching departure, there was a quiet and resolved confidence which showed supreme conviction of her safety, and prophesied, without presumption, the triumph over death. Of the dry and cold-blooded paganism which affects indifference to death, or the theory that it comes as a regular and legitimate sequence in a process fixed and ordained by natural law, and should therefore be accepted, or even welcomed with satisfaction by man—of that pernicious philosophical opinion she knew nothing save that it has no place in a Christian's convictions. The awe and dread of death were on her, as they are in all men and women of sound mind and just apprehension of our story and our doom: but the dread and awe were exorcised and cast out, not by any heathen speculation, but by the profound, the consoling, the glorious teachings of Catholic Eschatology, and by the light which it flings in full flood on the dark valley of the shadow of death. Jesus Christ is He to whom alone man may turn for help. Nay, it may be asked, who so near to Jesus Christ, so sensible of His Presence at the last, as they who have left all, in the literal and exact sense of the word, and are, body, soul, and spirit, one with Him, bound by one firm purpose which has overthrown all resistance, and by vows which have been kept faithfully to the end ? To whom shall we go but to Thee in Thy Life ? And where in death shall we go but to Thee ?

If there was one thought above all others habitual with her, it was that of the shortness of the time and the nearness of the end. On one All Souls' Day, when they visited the little sleeping place at Peekskill and laid flowers on the graves, she said : " I wonder whether I shall be resting here on the next All Souls' Day." In the latter year, the last of her life, when the care and the burden were becoming daily heavier and heavier, she wrote :

" I have been about writing you for some little time past, but somehow have not managed it : perhaps it was because I did not like writing about myself. I find myself obliged to lay down some laws in regard to the use of my one poor eye. I understand the doctor thinks a cataract is forming: this may or may not be so; but I am trying to get used to the thought that it may be so. I have given up general reading, only looking over a book or a paper just a little; and I have determined never to use a book except in the broad daylight, and to get as much help as possible in the way of letter-writing, etc., etc.; so if my letters are few the Sisters will know the cause. It may be that God intends to lay me aside for awhile in this world before I am taken to my Eternal Rest. Whatever His will be, may my will ever be His."

On occasion of another severe attack of illness toward the end, she wrote :

" I suppose you know why there has been no word from me all through our great Feast.*
. . . I was obliged to succumb and have the doctor sent for. Well, he kept me a prisoner in my bed for nine whole days *with no privileges ;* however, on the Octave Day I was allowed to be in the ante-chapel and make my communion, and I had the benefit of Second Vespers; but I am still in some sense a prisoner. I am allowed to be in my office for a time, and do some work, and to have my meals served me there, but I am not yet allowed to go down to the Refectory or the Community room. I know that it is necessary to be careful. The doctor feared that the inflammation would extend to the other lung, but it did not. I suppose I shall not be permitted to go to the city for some little time yet. There ! a long letter all about myself ! "

But why put off saying what now must follow ? It was near the end of Lent, in the year 1896; those weeks were at hand when the faithful watch Christ in His Passion, accompanying Him, step by step, on His way forth from this troubled world. Now, at the time more fit for the purpose than any other, the devout Religious at St. Gabriel's were called to watch the departure of their

* Referring to the Purification and its Octave.

beloved head from their company and her transit to the royal land of flowers and light. Everything seems to have been ordered by those higher intelligences to whom is committed the care of the children of Our Lord ; and great is the peace which fills the soul when we observe how all was brought about to that end.

No one was anticipating what occurred : it came suddenly and without warning. The Mother had been as well as usual, bright, and like herself, as one who might yet see many years. On Passion Sunday, March 22d, 1896, she was in the Chapel for the last time. The Rev. Dr. Riley, of the General Theological Seminary, had been conducting a Retreat: in his last meditation on the Love of God in our glorification, he had dwelt much on the life after death. The following Monday the Mother spoke to one of the Sisters on the subject, and told her what a rest and refreshment the Retreat had been to her, and what a pleasure it had been to receive more light on the subjects on which her mind had been dwelling of late ; adding that she felt as though she had had a glimpse into the unseen world, that the cares then pressing on her were lightened and easier to bear, or rather that she felt lifted above them. She went on to speak of the points in the meditation which had chiefly impressed her; and then she said: " I have been thinking a great deal of late about death and what it will mean to me personally ; but I cannot make it real ; I don't know at all how I shall feel when I know that I am to die."

That day she felt very tired and had a cold, but she was up part of the day. On Tuesday they wanted her to see the physician, but she refused, saying that she would soon be better and hoped to be quite well for Holy Week. On Wednesday, she was worse and consented to see the doctor ; apologizing to him for putting off sending for him on the ground that he had so many demands on his time and she did not wish to add one care more. He pronounced it a case of acute bronchitis, and seemed hopeful.

She was apparently comfortable during the remainder of Passion Week; quiet, and, as usual, deeply interested in school affairs, enquiring every morning about the girls, and particularly about two of the number in whom she was much occupied in thought about that time.

On Saturday a change occurred: it was pneumonia. When told so, she said : " I wonder if the Master has come for me"; and soon after she added, " I think God will ask me to give up going to the Chapel in Holy Week. I have never missed the Night Offices before; all of Lent I have been hoping that I could fully keep Holy Week."

Palm Sunday came ; and in the morning she told the Sister who had been with her constantly to leave her for a while, get her palm, and make her communion ; which she did. On returning she brought with her a palm for the Mother, and as she saw it placed over the picture of St. Theresa which always hung in her room, her eyes filled with tears, and she said : "It is the first time I have missed the Palm Service," adding, a few moments afterwards : "It is the will of God." When reminded that this was perhaps intended as her special Lenten discipline, she said : "Yes, this may be the Cross our dear Master wishes me to carry for Him and it is a very real one." The next day, when told that the Sisters were saying The Way of the Cross, she replied : "I too am saying the Way of the Cross."

During Holy Week the Mother took very little notice of what was going on ; she suffered much from restlessness, and asked not to be left alone, as she had troubled dreams and saw strange and dark things when she closed her eyes: she seemed however to suffer little pain. Her frequent request was for "water fresh from the well." On Maundy Thursday she received the Blessed Sacrament. It was brought to her from the Chapel; she had followed the service exactly and was told when the priest was beginning the Canon. After reception she remained perfectly calm and peaceful, murmuring to herself: "I am waiting; the Master has been served."

Often during those last hours she was heard to be saying, as if secretly : "Light, Emblem of Life"; and "Dear Master" ; and again, "He leadeth and guideth me," and "obedient unto death." On Thursday night she said aloud : "They are calling me," but gave no explanation.

On Good Friday when a very dear friend came from New York to see her, she rallied somewhat, roused herself and recognized him. Then unconsciousness returned: but it was felt by those who watched by her that it was only toward the side of earth, that this was a special preparation for the life beyond, and that already in heart and mind she had entered the world of the Unseen.

On Easter Even the Blessed Sacrament was administered to her for the last time.

On Easter Day after Matins in the Church, the

priest came and said the Commendatory Prayer : while he was doing so she fixed her eyes upon him and evidently knew what was going on. Thus the hours passed, until about 3 o'clock **P.M.** the Sisters were summoned and knelt about her. It was just before the hour of None. One of the Sisters was reading the Gradual Psalms, the rest responding. The Chapel bell rang out the ninth hour of the day. The Mother heard it, opened her eyes wide, and seemed to be looking into the other world. Then slightly lifting her hands, while the final prayers were said, she breathed out her soul without a struggle, and was with her Master.

On Thursday in Easter Week the body was reverently laid to rest. It is unnecessary to say more than has been already said in the Prelude about the scenes in the Chapel and the Cemetery that day. An account of the funeral services, the only one authorized by the Sisters, has been published as an appendix to a sermon preached by the Chaplain of the School on Low Sunday.* To

* Faith through Love. A sermon preached in St. Mary's Chapel, Peekskill, New York, on Low Sunday, 1896, being the first Sunday after the Burial of Sister Harriet, Foundress of the "Sisterhood of St. Mary, New

that account the reader is referred. Let me add but one thing : the hymn, a favourite of hers, which was sung as the priests who acted as bearers took the bier from the choir, and bore it away to the cemetery.

THE RETURN HOME.

" Safe Home! Safe home in port!
    Rent cordage, shattered deck,
Torn sails, provisions short,
    And only not a wreck;
But oh, the joy upon the shore,
To tell our voyage perils o'er!

" The prize, the prize secure!
    The athlete nearly fell;
Bare all he could endure,
    And bare not always well:
But he may smile at troubles gone
Who puts the victor-garland on!

" The lamb is in the fold
    In perfect safety penn'd;
The lion once had hold,
    And thought to make an end.
But One came by with wounded side,
And for the sheep the Shepherd died.

York," and for thirty-two years its Mother Superior. By the Rev. Arthur Lowndes, D.D. To which is added an authorized account of the Funeral Services on the Thursday in Easter Week. New York, James Pott & Co., Publishers, Fourth Avenue and 22d St. 1896.

" No more the foe can harm:
    No more of leaguer'd camp,
And cry of night alarm,
    And need of ready lamp:
And yet how nearly had he failed,—
How nearly had that foe prevail'd !

" The exile is at home!—
    Oh, nights and days of tears,
Oh, longings not to roam,
    Oh, sins and doubts and fears,—
What matter now, when (so men say)
The King has wip'd those tears away?

" O happy, happy Bride!
    Thy widow'd hours are past,
The Bridegroom at thy side,
    Thou all His Own at last!
The sorrows of thy former cup
In full fruition swallow'd up!"

.   .   .   .

ÆTERNA FAC CUM SANCTIS TUIS IN GLORIA
NUMERARI.

10

CONCLUSION.

M Y task is completed; and now, with a full knowledge of its unworthiness and imperfections, her old friend reverently lays this offering upon that grave wherein her mortal body is sleeping in peace. It has been a help and a relief to spend so much time during the past summer in this communing with the holy dead. These pages were written in part by the sea-shore where the grey Atlantic spreads its waste of waters, often veiled in fog and mist, and still beating out their perpetual chime against the grassy dunes; in part on the banks of the lovely St. Regis lake, where the tall pines lift their solemn shafts and foliage to the sky, and the mountains, changing with every hour, announce, as of old, the righteousness of the Eternal. In either place, there was pause from the confusing nosies and uproar of these troubled and anxious months; brief respite from the din made by the enemies to our peace and to the good order of society, the noisy orator, the political agitator, the stirrer of strife among brethren, the new woman of the period, the prophets of evil, and those who deem it their mission to upset, subvert, and destroy the landmarks set by our fathers. When the world seems in throes, as about to bring forth one knows not what new and monstrous progeny, and when the hearts of men are failing them for fear and for looking for those things which are coming on the earth ; it may be counted a privilege beyond estimate to have been drawn, either by the sense of obligation or by the strength of a deep attachment, or in any other way, to lengthened communion with an unworldly and exalted soul, to have been permitted to watch a star of God shining more and more unto the perfect day; and while musing of a life rooted and grounded in love, strong in reverence for the things eternal, devoted to God, and liberally provident of the best gifts that can be had here below, to have forgotten meanwhile, or ceased to observe that there are anywhere about us persons without religion and without grace, whose lives are led outside the Kingdom, the centre of whose thoughts, desires, and hopes is in a world which decays and is ready to vanish away. And now, gentle reader, that we have meditated together on this precious story, let it be asked, whether we can do anything to express gratitude and appreciation, if the narrative has awakened them with-

in our spirit ?   What permanent memorial should
there be of the first Mother Superior of the largest
of our American Sisterhoods ?   Let this suggestion be made : that, by many offerings of love,
from many warm hearts and many hands, there
be erected in time on the place where she dwelt
and where her body rests, a Mother House, apt
and meet in all respects to be the dwelling of the
Community.   Let us arise and build, to the glory
of God and to the memory of His devoted daughter.   Perhaps this little narrative may meet the
eye of some woman whose heart is in the world,
whose life has little else to show but a round of
self-seeking and amusement in society.   Were it
not well for her to look on such a life as this, and
by some timely offering establish a sympathetic
relation with one, side by side with whom she
must finally meet her Judge ?   It is possible that
these pages may be read by some one of the
women of the advanced school, who, doubtless
with an intention which seems to them to justify
that course, devote their best power to the demo-
lition of that ideal of womanhood, which only,
thus far, has helped and blessed the world ?
Might not the heart of such a one be reached and
softened, by seeing what good was done by a great,
earnest, loving spirit working on the old lines,

true to that womanly model which we reverence in the Church and honour with " all but adoring love " in the Blessed Mother of our Lord Jesus Christ ? Howsoever it be, let us arise, bring presents, and offer gifts. It is memorable, and as true as strange, that not one woman rich in this world's goods has ever cast in her lot with this Community : their recruits have come from the ranks of those who were rich in faith alone. It is time that others in a different position recognize a privilege here which, once seen, will be gladly acknowledged. Great as was the work of their first Mother Superior, we trust that the Sisterhood of St. Mary are to see greater things than these, and that the light now shining in their houses shall shine more and more for many generations after we have vanished from sight.